GEEKY BOYS, FREAKY BOYS

An Erotic Anthology

Edited By

Mickey Erlach

STAR BOOKS PRESS

Herndon, VA

Published in the United States by STARbooks Press, PO Box 711612, Herndon, VA 20171. Printed in the United States

Many thanks to graphic artist John Nail for the cover design.

Mr. Nail may be reached at: tojonail@bellsouth.net.

Herndon, VA

STARbooks Press Titles Edited by Mickey Erlach

CONTENTS

CONTENTS

TIED IN KNOTS
By Michael Turner

Michael Turner lives in South Wales, UK, with his partner and a mad Springer Spaniel. He divides his time between writing, painting, and walking the dog. E-mail him at galadann100@gmail.com.

"Don't look now, but he's coming over," my best friend, Tom, said quietly.

We were sitting in the canteen of our university hall trying to enjoy a quiet Saturday morning breakfast, which was easier said than done. A group of us, Tom included, had hit the town hard the night before, and we were suffering from hangovers from hell.

The canteen wasn't helping either. Every noise from the tinkling of the cutlery to the whirring of the coffee machine ground on my nerves until I was sure my head was going to explode. The chatter of the other students permeated the air like the ruckus cawing of seagulls.

Only the thought of sausages, the meat variety and not the human kind, had dragged me from my pit of a bed – and the thought that the swimming team always had breakfast together every Saturday usually dressed in nothing more than flimsy vests and those long, figure-hugging athletic leggings that left very little to the imagination. Tom lived off campus, and I'd promised him I'd take him to breakfast, so he could enjoy the sight, too.

For some reason I hadn't really expected to see Taylor, which was stupid seeing as he was captain of the swimming team. I looked up and watched him walk across the canteen. He was wearing a white singlet top that revealed his musculature beautifully. Looking at him, you could see the inspiration for Michelangelo's David.

On his lower half, he wore the ubiquitous swimming team leggings – royal blue with two white stripes down the outside. The trousers hugged his body revealing his thin waist, thick thighs and a bulge no amount of material could disguise.

I groaned as his beautiful green eyes caught mine. "I can't face this now," I whispered to Tom. I'd had a crush on Taylor ever since I'd accidentally bumped into him in the canteen a year ago. I'd made a fool of myself then as I'd tried to apologize for covering him in orange juice and trying to clean him up. Mortified was a good word for how I'd felt at that time. He was gracious enough to laugh it off and that had been that … for him.

For me, it was the start of a stupid infatuation. I attended every swim team training session, sitting high up in the stadium in the shadows where no one would see me. I'd attended every home competition and even those away, sometimes travelling halfway across the country. It was a deluded fantasy on my part. Taylor was straight and totally manly straight. He had a girlfriend whom he had been seeing for over a year and rumor had it that he didn't play away at all. When I'd made the mistake of finally approaching him to ask him out he'd laughed in my face. Before the end of the day, it was all over campus what a fool I'd been.

Not content with punishing myself by attending swim meets to see him, I discovered the day I walked into my law class that he was also on that part of my course. He sat two rows in front of me in the lecture theatre which allowed me unfettered ogling of his broad, muscular shoulders for that one hour each week.

"Hi," said Taylor smiling as he came to a stop before our table drawing me from my thoughts. Tom and I looked up together. He was smiling broadly at us. "Mind if I take a seat?"

I shrugged. "If you want." Being this close to him had me tongue-tied, and my hangover wasn't helping. Even though this was Taylor, the man of my dreams, and featured star of practically all my jerk off fantasies, I just wanted to be left alone.

It wasn't to be. He sat down next to Tom and beamed at the pair of us. "You boys look as if you had a good night," he said in what I was certain was a normal voice but seemed to be shouting to me.

"Mind keeping the noise down a bit," I muttered, trying to focus on him, my eyes still bleary. I guessed my eyes must be bloodshot. What a state to finally get close to him in.

Taylor chuckled, the sound mellifluous and strangely relaxing. "Oh boy, it must have been a good one." He grinned as I threw him a sarcastic smile.

"What do you want?" I asked, a little abruptly.

His grin faltered, and I guess I must have come across rude. "Sorry," I whispered.

"No problem." His grin returned. "I was wondering what you were doing tomorrow?"

I knew what a rabbit felt like trapped in the headlights. "Nothing. Why?"

"Umm ..." He looked down at the table suddenly reluctant to say whatever it as he had come to say.

"Taylor," I said sharply, "I have a splitting headache, and I can do without all this ..." I waved, at a loss for words. "Just say whatever it is you came to say."

He took a deep breath and rooted around in the rucksack he had brought with him. When he surfaced, he handed over a strip of paracetamols. "These might help," he said quietly as he pushed them across the table to me.

At that moment, my heart went out to him, and I could have kissed him right there in the middle of the canteen ... to be honest I could do that anytime so that wasn't a new feeling for me. "Thanks," I croaked, my throat tight as I shoved two of the tablets toward Tom who accepted them greedily.

Knocking back two, I took huge swig of my orange juice and swallowed the tablets before focusing on Taylor again. "So what's up?" I asked.

He took another deep breath. "You're in my law class, right?" I nodded. "I'm kinda having trouble there. I don't seem to understand half of whatever Professor Maddison is saying." I waited wondering where this was going. He sighed. "To be honest I'm near to failing the class."

That was a surprise to me. I was certain Taylor would excel at everything he did. I assumed he sailed through his coursework either because he was intelligent and could do it or because the lecturers went easy on him as he was on the swim team – most places are still sport over learning even though our glorious institutions refute that.

"Everyone knows you excel in law. I was wondering if …. you'd be willing to give me a little tutoring. Just to help me get through the next assignment."

"No," I said before I could think. "You must think I'm a real idiot." Taylor had the grace to look sheepish. "After what you did to me that time, why in hell's name would I want to help you? You caused me untold hours of embarrassment and grief."

Taylor nodded. "I know, but I was forced into the position by the boys on the swim team."

"Bollocks," I snarled. "It was you boasting about the fag who just couldn't leave you alone." Taylor looked ashamed and hung his head slightly. "No way am I going to help you. I don't care if you do fail the course."

Taylor's beautiful green eyes narrowed. "You're even more of a bitch than they say you are," he spat. "Fine, be that way." I watched him storm off even then unable to not admire his pert backside.

I looked at Tom. He shrugged. "What?" My head was starting to pound as if a team of ten-ton elephants were practicing a ballet routine.

"You were kinda harsh," he said.

"He deserves it."

Tom nodded thoughtfully. "I agree what he did was wrong, but that would have been your perfect opportunity to have him indebted to you. Might have been useful."

All day I thought about what Tom had said … and the fact that the gossip mill had me pegged as a bitch. It was true I'd done all I could to get back at Taylor in the aftermath of my embarrassment, and some of it hadn't been too above board but I'd been hurting and looking back … well I was wrong.

Swallowing my pride later that evening, I entered the halls where Taylor lived. I nodded to the guard on duty who smirked at me and winked back – no doubt remembering the blowjob I'd given him, which he said was vastly better than his wife's attempts, as I headed to the stairs and climbed to the third floor.

I knew exactly which was Taylor's room; I'd stalked him long enough to find out the basics. When I got there I took a deep breath and knocked on the door.

It opened immediately as if Taylor had been waiting. My breath caught in my throat. He was naked apart from a towel wrapped around his waist. Droplets of water glistened on his muscular chest; his muscles working beneath his smooth skin as he toweled; his brown hair made even darker by the water.

I couldn't stop my eyes from travelling south following the ridges of muscle, which made up his six pack until they hit the small trail of dark brown hair which fanned out beneath his belly button. My cock stirred as it too noticed the Greek God before me.

"What?" he demanded roughly, glaring at me which I guessed I deserved.

"Can we talk?" I asked quietly after moistening my lips.

Taylor shrugged and stepped back into the room. His roommate was asleep on the bed in the far corner. Taking another deep breath, I began. "I'm sorry, for the way I acted earlier." Taylor shrugged and just watched me. "You made me feel like shit those few weeks after I told you how I felt, and I was hung over and tired, and I just snapped." I paused. "I'm sorry."

Taylor nodded. "Okay, fine. Apology accepted. If that's it, can you excuse me? I have to get dressed."

"No that's not all," I said tamping down the desire to snarl at him. "If you still want tutoring for your law assignment I'll do it but ..."

His green eyes lit up but were tinged with suspicion." "But what?"

"But I want paying."

"Oh, I'm on a grant here," he said softly, "I don't have any spare cash." The light in his beautiful green eyes died along with something in me; the bitterness and rage for all he'd put me through went with it.

"That's okay," I said, "There are more ways to pay than just money." I winked at him.

The color drained from his face. "I'm straight."

"I know," I replied with a lopsided grin on my face, "but I've always wanted to do it with a straight man and now may be my chance." I didn't tell him that he had been seen in the gay club in the city fifty miles from campus three weekends in a row, or the fact that he'd been dancing and enjoying himself, and I certainly didn't mention the fact that I'd actually watched him kiss a man openly on the dance floor.

Taylor swallowed, his eyes darting from side to die as if seeking an exit. He licked his lips.

"Anyway," I said, "the offer's there. I'll be in my room until ten." I glanced at my watch. "It's only seven now. It's up to you. I'm not forcing you or anything." I shrugged, took one last look at his perfect physique and left.

Sitting in my room I watched the clock go from seven until eight then nine. At nine-thirty I sighed heavily certain Taylor wasn't coming. I knew it had been a long shot, but I still felt disappointed.

Mixing myself a cocktail I chuckled thinking this was probably the closest I was going it get to sex on the beach this year. Stirring the mixture, I watched the red grenadine swirl into the orange juice anticipating the sweet taste and the hit of vodka that would follow.

A gentle tap on my door pulled me out of my thoughts, and I glanced at the clock to see there were still ten minutes to go before the ultimate deadline. My breath caught in my throat. Could it be Taylor? Had he finally taken up my offer?

I opened the door, my heart in my throat. Acute disappointment followed, and I plummeted, my hopes dashed again. It was stupid of me to let them be raised; I berated myself as I stood looking at my law professor.

He grinned at me. "Bet you didn't expect to see me," he teased.

"Not at ten o'clock in the night," I said before my mind engaged.

"True. It is late," he replied. "I was just passing and I wanted to give this back to you." I took the paper he offered me, recognizing my latest law assignment. "Your

9

arguments were brilliant," he said enthusiastically, "but I'll talk to you about it again." His eyes darted to his left around the corner where I couldn't see. "I think you may have company," he whispered as he waved and walked off.

I frowned and leaned out of my door trying to find the source of his comment. My eyes locked on a pair of emerald green orbs full of trepidation and fear. "Hi," said Taylor quietly, shifting from foot to foot like a nervous rabbit. I was sure he would dart away at any second.

"Hi. Come in," I said equally soft, backing into my room.

Taylor followed cautiously, his eyes roaming around taking in every detail of my small room. He jumped visibly when I closed the door, the lock clicking loudly into place in the ensuing silence.

"Can I get you a drink?"

Taylor swallowed before answering. "What's that?" he asked pointing at my cocktail.

"Sex on the Beach," I answered immediately, grinning at his discomfort. "Vodka and peach schnapps and orange juice."

He licked his lips nervously, not realizing the effect he was having on me. My jeans had suddenly become tighter, and my cock was trapped painfully, throbbing like it was trying to send Morse code.

10

"You came then," I said handing over his drink. "I didn't think you were going to show up."

"I nearly didn't," he sipped his drink as he sat on the edge of my mattress. Jumping up immediately as if it had bitten him, he moved to the chair behind my desk instead. "This is good." He held up the cocktail.

"What changed your mind?"

"I need a decent law grade; otherwise I'm gone."

I saw the lost look in his eyes and suddenly I felt like shit. All the times he'd embarrassed me flashed through my mind and as bad as they were they didn't really compare to what I was doing to him.

I sighed heavily and watched my evening of having sex with the man I'd idolized for ages flying off into the distance. I couldn't do this to him. "Taylor, relax." My voice was soft and quiet trying to calm him. "You don't have to do anything you don't want to. I didn't realize this would affect you so badly. We can just have a drink and call it quits at that and ... I'll help you with your assignment."

Taylor's green orbs went wide, then narrowed shrewdly. "Why?" he asked. "Why would you do that for me?"

"I've been a shit to you trying to get you to do this. For what it's worth, I'm sorry."

Taylor looked at me calculatingly and finally visibly relaxed. Glancing over to the bed his eyes went wide

11

again, and the tension returned. "What the hell are those?" He pointed to the bed posts.

I closed my eyes and groaned. I'd forgotten about the black leather restraints I'd attached to the bed in preparation. I took a deep breath, opened my eyes and shrugged. "I have a fetish," I said with a mixture of apology and defiance.

Taylor relaxed again, his beautiful green eyes that I found so intoxicating turning curious. "You like getting tied up?"

I shrugged. "I don't mind it, but I prefer doing the tying up.

His eyes went wide again. For someone so popular amongst the ladies, he wasn't half doing a brilliant job of having his innocence stripped away ... unless it wasn't an act, maybe he'd never come across restraints and leather before although given his place as a male icon in the university I found that hard to believe.

"You were planning on tying me to the bed?" he stuttered, licking his lips nervously.

I nodded.

"Were you planning on fucking me, too?"

I shook my head quickly. "No. Don't get me wrong I'd love to be inside your hot arse, but I wasn't planning on it for tonight. I'm guessing you've never had anything up there, and the first time can be quite painful, and despite what you may think, I have no desire to hurt you."

Taylor's eyes travelled between the bed, tracing all four restraints and my eyes and then back to the bed. "So ... what were you planning?"

"Does it really matter?" I asked with a sigh. "You don't want to be here, not for this anyway, and I've agreed to give you a hand with your assignments already. There's no need to go over this."

Taylor pinned me with his stare. "Tell me," he said, his voice taking on a commanding tone, then more quietly and gently, "please."

I sighed. I seemed to be doing a lot of that around him lately – just a shame it was in the wrong way. "I was going to tie you to the bed and then straddle you and ride your cock until you came." I felt my face flame at the admission.

"Why the restraints?" Taylor moved to the bed and picked up the loose end of one of the leather straps attached to the headboard, turning it over and examining it.

"I was afraid you'd run, and I didn't want you to go until you were finished," I admitted, watching his sensual hands handle the leather over and over.

Taylor looked over his shoulder at me. "Aren't you supposed to have a safe word or something?"

My brows rose. Maybe he wasn't as innocent as I believed. I nodded.

Taylor turned back to the restraint and laid it back on the mattress. He nodded to himself as if making a decision then turned and stood before me. "What word shall we use?" he asked softly.

A calm descended on the room as if a snowstorm had struck, and we were the only people left after it had blown itself out. I stared at him, stunned, unable to believe I'd heard what he said or unsure to believe what it meant.

After a few seconds he shrugged and moved for the door. "Well if you don't want to."

His movement spurred me to life, and I grabbed his wrist as he passed me. His skin was soft and smooth and warm, and my cock jumped in my jeans at the touch. "Wait," I practically screamed, the sound loud in the quiet room. "Of course I want to," I said moderating my tone, "you just took me by surprise."

Taylor looked at me. "How about cauliflower?"

"Cauliflower?"

Taylor grinned back at me. His face was alive and open and full of warmth, his eyes sparkling. I'd not seen him smile around me much, and it was a pleasure to behold. It seemed to enhance his good looks, and my heart fluttered. Forcing back the feelings that were swamping me, I tried to ignore them as I realized he had me all tied in knots – pun intended.

14

"Can't imagine I'll be saying that much when we're … you know."

I laughed, and he joined me, his voice warm and rich and deep. "You can say fucking, you know," I teased.

"So how do we go about this," he asked, nodding.

"Well there are the birds and the bees," I started slowly, my tone soft and explanatory, "although in this case there are no birds and two bees."

"Funny," he grinned at me, the back of his hand slapping my chest softly.

Suddenly my mouth was dry as the realization dawned on me that Taylor was in my room, we were laughing together and discussing fucking. "How about you lose your clothes?" I suggested.

Taylor's green eyes flashed with mirth. "I thought you'd never ask." He reached for the bottom of his T-shirt pulling the material up over his head and tossing it aside in one go.

Unable to stop myself, my eyes raked his torso. His skin was tanned a soft golden brown from the early summer sunshine we'd been experiencing, and his muscles rippled seductively beneath his smooth skin.

His shoulders were broad and muscular supporting his well-developed pectoral muscles, which were topped with two nubs of flesh that stood out hard and firm. Apart from the small trail of hair below his navel that led beneath

15

the tight waistband of his narrow jeans, his torso was hairless, and I assumed, rightly or wrongly, that he shaved it to make himself more aerodynamic in the water.

Taylor grinned shyly at me, and I had a sudden realization that there was a shy man hiding beneath all the bluster and bravado he normally exuded. "Okay?" he asked.

"Fuck yeah!" I almost shouted. "You're gorgeous." I blushed furiously at my admission.

Taylor chuckled quietly in an endearing way. "You've seen all this before. I know you've been to practically every swim meet I've had in uni."

I nodded. "Not practically. I've been to them all, but I've never been this close to you in such a state of undress before." I couldn't stop my eyes from raking his body over and over, ogling his smooth muscles.

"You're gonna make my head grow," he said laughing.

"It already has," I replied pointedly starring at his groin where the bulge was getting bigger and materializing into a visible erection.

Without another word, Tyler unbuckled his belt and popped his fly giving me a tantalizing glimpse of his 2xist underwear. The white of the material contrasted nicely with the tan of his skin, and I unconsciously licked my lips.

Toeing off his boots, it wasn't long before his jeans followed the way of his T-shirt, and he stood before me in nothing but his underwear. The man was akin to a Greek God with muscles bulging everywhere. His legs were like the rest of him, sleek and powerful and designed for propelling him through the water – everything about him seemed calculated to either improve his sportsmanship or his physique. It was all I could do to keep my raging hormones in check and not ravage him there and then – especially once I spotted his thick thighs.

With a cheeky grin that I was beginning to find adorable, Taylor threw himself on my bed, landing with a bounce that made his legs spread wide giving me a fantastic view up the 'V' of his legs straight to his groin where his underwear was tenting in front of him.

Mentally shaking myself I pulled myself together and moved into action. Bending over I reached for the first restraint taking the piece of leather in one hand and his wrist in the other. Taylor licked his lips, and I felt the tremor which ran though him.

I stopped. "Taylor? Are you sure about this?"

He smiled nervously as he nodded. "Yup. I'm just a little scared, I guess."

"I'm not going to hurt you, and you have 'cauliflower' after all."

He grinned at me. "Strap me up and let's get going." His green eyes flashed at me, his muscles heaving as he took a deep breath, mentally I heard his unspoken 'before I change my mind.'

17

Taking him at his word, I buckled the strap around his wrist tight enough so that he could feel it but not tight enough to cut off his circulation. I quickly strapped his other wrist to the bed immobilizing him.

Stepping back, I gazed down at him. Taylor had closed his eyes, so I couldn't read his green orbs to see how he was feeling, but he was breathing normally, and there didn't seem to be any tension through his body, quite the opposite in fact. He seemed relaxed and supine.

That all changed when I reached for his briefs. As I gripped the waistband, his eyes flew open. "Stop," he said urgently. "Can't you leave those on?"

"Well I could, but I'm not going to." I grabbed his waistband and pulled, peeling the white cotton down over his handsome thighs and calves. I wanted him feeling vulnerable enough to know his place but not scared enough that he'd shout "cauliflower."

Taylor's cock slapped against his belly with an audible smack bouncing back to stand upright, proud and tall. My mouth went dry at the sight of his gorgeous manhood. It was at least eight inches in length and as thick as a cola bottle. A wide blue vein snaked around the shaft like a meandering river winding its way down until it disappeared into his dark pubic hair. My eyes were dragged down to where his low hanging balls the size of plums swung heavy with their precious load. His slit was already leaking pre-cum and the spicy scent of man-musk was beginning to permeate the air.

Reaching out, I quickly strapped his ankles to the bed posts, spreading his legs wide giving me access to his most sacred of areas. I looked up in time to catch his green orbs staring at me. They were hooded as if he was beginning to zone out. "Taylor?" I asked a little worried.

He looked at me and grinned. "I'm guessing you're liking what you see," he teased, nodding at my groin where my own stiff cock was tapped painfully in my jeans tenting the denim material.

"Too right," I grinned back, crossing the room to my wardrobe where I hauled out a large steel box. Opening the lid, I reached in and pulled out a gag. Hiding it behind my back I crossed back to Taylor who was straining to try to see what I was doing.

Holding up the ball with the leather straps attached, giving him a clear view, I said, "Gag or not?"

Taylor's beautiful eyes went comically wide, like a cartoon character's before they turned smoky and smoldering. "Will you be able to understand 'cauliflower' with that in?"

"Of course," I replied. "I may be a gangly geek, but I'm very practiced at this. Don't worry. I'm not going to hurt you."

Taylor eyed the gag warily and then nodded. "With," he said, his voice deep and husky. "And you're not gangly or a geek," he added quickly. "You're ... lean and very smart."

"Whatever," I grinned, pleased with his comments as I reached forward and popped the leather ball into his mouth and buckled the straps behind his head. "Okay?"

Taylor nodded.

"Want a blindfold, or shall we save that for another time?"

His eyes went wide again, and he immediately shook his head. "No worries," I replied as I began to shuck my clothing, stripping down to bare skin in seconds. My cock, like Taylor's was rearing and ready to go. It was so hard I thought it was going to burst out of its skin, and I kept mentally telling myself that I wasn't fucking today, but mini-me wasn't taking any notice.

Reaching out, I tentatively grasped Taylor's shaft and ran my hand down the silky smooth skin. He was as hard to the touch as he looked, his rod red hot and throbbing. I ran my hand right to the root, my fist delving through his soft pubic hair. Closing my fingers, I gripped and squeezed tight delighted when Taylor groaned loudly. My other hand strayed to his balls and gripped them, hefting them in my palm, enjoying the feel of their weight.

My breathing increased, and my cock throbbed, a bead of pre-cum escaping from my slit. I'd not been this revved up in a while. There was something about Taylor besides his gorgeous muscular body that got to me. It might have been his sensual animal magnetism or his lithe physicality, but I was finding myself wondering just how long it would be before I shot my load.

I ran my hand up and down his hot flesh pole enjoying the sensations from the heat and his smooth skin, rubbing my thumb over his flaring head and cumslit. Taylor groaned and jerked his hips into my hand, and I had the urge to edge him, to watch his handsome face distort in sexual pleasure.

My cock jumped, and another huge drop of pre-cum oozed out falling to the bed in a long trail. My groans joined Taylor's. I reached for the lube and condom determined to get Taylor in me before I came in case I didn't get another chance. This was supposed to be a one off and I wasn't certain how Taylor was going to react once I freed him. I was hoping he would enjoy himself and want to come back for more again and again, but all gay men know when a closet case or a curious straight man surfaces from the depths of sensual ecstasy, their reaction is anything but predictable.

With deft practiced moves and accompanied by Taylor's groan, I rolled a condom down his solid shaft and slicked it up with lube. He moaned repeatedly as my fist ran up and down him, coating him. He felt so good, I couldn't resist jerking him a few times more than was absolutely necessary.

Through fluttering eyelashes, he watched me, his green orbs drinking in every detail. My cock throbbed as I watched him. He looked so beautiful, his arms tied to the bed, his mouth gagged, that I almost shot my load before I got anywhere near him.

Breathing deeply, I managed to get myself back under control. My fear of shooting before I could get any fun resurfaced, and I quickly threw my leg over his waist, straddling his hips and grinning at him, my cock bobbing in his line of sight.

He swallowed hard as his eyes followed my member. Reaching back, I grasped his hard prick and guided him to the entrance to my most sacred of places.

Taylor whimpered as I pressed the tip of his cock against my sphincter. I smiled reassuringly down at him and slowly sat back. I watched his eyes widen as my ring gripped his cockhead and began to slide over it. White hot heat engulfed his sensitive glans as his cock began to disappear into me.

Pushing backwards, I pressed hard repeatedly forcing his head into my hole until my defenses admitted defeat, and he slipped into me.

Taylor groaned loud and long, his green eyes never leaving mine. I grinned at him and reached for my own straining cock, which was leaving a trail a pre-cum over his flat belly as it bobbed up and down.

I was hard and rearing to go. My hand felt good as it ran up and down my shaft, my thumb swiping my sensitive head.

Taking a deep breath, I shoved backwards, and Taylor's cock filled me, stretching my hole and filling my tunnel. It felt as if he was going to go on and on forever. His eight inches felt like miles of hard muscle shoving into me, like a rod of heat deep in my core.

Eventually, I settled my butt cheeks on his thighs, his hairs tickling me. I let out a deep breath that I hadn't been aware I was holding and grinned at him again, my hands steadying me, gripping his torso.

I breathed deeply, waiting for the pain to subside, which I knew it would. I squirmed around on his thick cock as I waited hoping the slight movement would help. Taylor's flexing of his mighty man muscle – little tiny stretches of my muscles until the pain receded and was soon replaced by an altogether different sensation.

Reaching forward, I pinched his nipples between my thumb and forefinger until he was squealing around the ball gag and arching his back as far off the bed as he could, inadvertently thrusting his cock balls deep into me.

Taking pity on him, I released his tender nubs of flesh, staying where I was as he sank back to the mattress allowing his cock to withdraw until only his wide flaring head remained inside me until I slammed myself back into his lap, driving his eight inches deep into me again.

Without pausing, I rose up and slammed down again. Over and over I began to ride Taylor hard, slamming him into me repeatedly, my knees gripping his flanks tight. I groaned as I angled my downward thrust slightly – his cockhead brushing past my prostate sending ecstasy through my system.

Taylor matched my groans as he began to thrust his hips forward pressing his dick into me, meeting my downward thrust, his reticence disappearing as the need of his manhood took over.

23

The slap of skin on skin filled the air echoing around the room, mixing with our panting breaths as we moved faster and faster, driving each other toward orgasm. Even though he looked as sexy as all hell, I wished I hadn't tied Taylor to the bed. I wanted to feel his hands on my body, stroking over my sensitive muscles; I wanted to feel his fist grip my cock tightly and jack me as I rode him. I just wanted to feel his touch.

My thoughts were driven away as Taylor began to whimper, his cries becoming more and more frantic as I forced his cock to pound me over and over. His eyes grew wider and wider in desperation as he neared his explosion, but I carried on. I wanted him to come in me but not before I'd come for him.

Grabbing my own leaking prick, I ran my hand up and down my solid shaft shivering at the ecstasy, which passed through me. With Taylor smashing into my prostate regularly and my stimulating my own cock, I knew my own release wasn't far away.

As if on cue, the tingling that I knew announced my release began on the base of my balls, and my orbs began their climb up my ropes. I beat my meat faster, matching Taylor's pace as he slammed my hole. I was going to be sore the next day from all the activity, but it was certainly going to be worth it.

My orbs locked onto Taylor's green eyes, and we watched avidly as we drove each other over the top.

With a loud scream I came, my cum bursting from the tip of my cock in long white ropes, splattering on his heaving chest. My muscles tensed and gripped his cock in a vice that caused him to groan long and hard and then with a grin in his green eyes, he came.

I could feel him emptying his load into the condom, throb after throb delivering his life giving seed, causing pleasure to the both of us. The sudden reservoir of heat in my backside spoke volumes for the amount he'd come, and once again I found myself regretting having tied him up. I would have liked to watch him shoot his load.

With a cheeky grin, I let myself fall forward lying on Taylor's well-muscled, manly chest. My cum squishing between us. We were both panting hard, sweat coating our bodies, Taylor letting out little whimpers.

After a few minutes of recovery, I pulled up slowly, raising my butt until with an audible plop his cock slipped from my well stretched hole. Taylor let out a long deep groan and smiled around the gag at me. Grinning back, I leaned forward, reached behind his head and released the strap holding the gag in place.

Taylor worked his jaw and then grinned at me. "That was fantastic," he whispered. "I've never felt anything like it." There was a contented glow surrounding him. I responded to him grinning broadly, running my hand up and down his chest and stomach muscles.

"Can we ..." Taylor licked his lips tentatively, "can we do it again? Without the restraints? I enjoyed being tied up and would love to do it again, but I'd like to do it where I can ... touch you, too."

I grinned openly down at him as I reached to untie his arms. "Of course we can," I replied. "Let's get cleaned up a bit, and then we can go again."

KNOW HOW I KNOW YOU'RE GAY
By Travis D. Boothe

Travis D. Boothe resides in North Carolina. He has had many short stories published and has most recently published his first full-length erotic novel, THE TRUTH ABOUT LIES. He can be reached at TravisBoothe33@gmail.com.

"I never really thought about us – together like this, but ..." Martin watched in awe and amazement as the thick, heart-shaped set of lips above him formed those words with a deep southern drawl.

"I ain't even trying to bullshit you; all I been able to do is think about you and me like this," Martin admitted, trying to force his own deep drawl past the dry lump in his nervous throat.

"Well, I ain't going to bullshit you, neither; you got a nigguh ready to try something new; know-I-mean?" The chunk of muscles that lay on top of Martin, trying not to smother his slender, one-thirty-two-pound body, leaned him back and pressed his shoulders flat on the mattress. The big, strong hands removed the glasses from his face. The thick, pink lips that Martin had been admiring just seconds earlier were now pressed against Martin's own thick, moist lips. Martin could feel the gentle scratch of the man's mustache against his own smooth upper lip. He could feel his own young cock swell and stiffen as the gorgeous beast above him forced their crotches into contact over and over again, his mammoth hands roaming Martin's body with the same intensity that his hungry mouth and his straining cock possessed. Martin shuttered as the huge hands came to a standstill upon reaching his hairless, chestnut brown ass cheeks.

"I ain't never done this before," Martin nervously disclosed. He teasingly ran his pedicured foot up his companion's thick calves, up to his tight thighs, and unto his equally well-sculpted bubble ass. "So you need to go easy at first."

"Me neither, but I got you, baby. Just trust me. I'm going to make it feel good; all you got to do is let me in."

"AHHHHGH!" Martin trembled as he felt the enormous head press against his super tight hole.

"Trust me baby; I won't make it hurt. Just open up!"

"OPEN UP!!!" The last two words of that phrase seemed to echo all around Martin, causing unrest to settle upon him, maybe because those words were accompanied by a frantic pounding noise. Someone was at the door to his room. He realized that he was indeed dreaming of the heap of muscles and the beastly cock that was lined up with his virgin pucker. Thank God!

He opened his eyes and felt around for his glasses. The one thing from the dream that remained was the lump

28

in his throat. He threw the covers from his bed and realized that sweat cascaded all over his naked body. His heart beat faster than that of a rabbit on crack-cocaine.

Jesus, had he really just dreamed of sex with another man, and why the hell was his cock still rigid and hard from the dream, etching its way out of the waistband of his boxers, pooling precum all over his smooth stomach? He adjusted it, hiding it down the leg of his baggy boxers as best he could. He threw his half-sleep legs over the side of the bed, heading towards the pounding noise at door.

"We know you're in there!" he could hear his friend, Ahmil, yell. "Stop playing with yourself and let us in, bitch! I told you, no matter how much you pull on it, it ain't going to get no longer!"

Martin started to verbally retaliate, but then a more devilish thought overtook his mind. He etched the waist of his underwear down in the back, until the band cut into the supple underside of his cheeks, causing them to rise, and to look more bodacious than usual, which was not Martin's intent. He turned his backside to the door, then twisted his waist around enough to allow his hands access to the latch. "Come in," he sang, turning again to spread his hairless cheeks apart. He wanted the first thing Ahmil saw when he came into the room to be his winking brown eye.

"Fucking faggot!" Ahmil yelped, doubling back into the hall. He shook his head as if the image of Martin's spread ass had scarred him for life.

Kareem, who had been accompanying Ahmil didn't give the same reaction. He stood, not able to tear his light green eyes from the surprise. He tried to hide the delight in them as Martin spun around laughing. Kareem hoped that his light beige skin didn't betray his thug nature by blushing bright red before his friends.

"My bad, Kareem; I didn't know you were out here, too." Martin held out his hands to give the boy dap, and Kareem accepted, as if he had not just seen the same hand that he was being offered used to pry Martin's asshole apart seconds earlier.

"We need a favor from you," Kareem informed. "The air conditioner is out on the other side of the dorm, and you got this big ass private room. Me and Ahmil want to crash in here with you for the night."

Martin decided that it would be pointless to ask if they were fucking serious, especially since they had come with pillows and blankets in hand. Instead, he stepped aside and motioned for them to come in. As annoying and intrusive as the situation seemed, he knew the two would do the same for him if the tables ever turned.

The two entered and literally basked in the sensation of the cool air, Ahmil even stripping from his sweat soaked tank-top and bowing before the air conditioning unit in appreciation. "Me and Kareem was over in our hot ass room dying, son!" he informed Martin. "Then it dawned on me that you over here with this huge ass room, and I know you too scared to take advantage of the location and sneak no pussy in, so I knew you were by yourself." Ahmil gazed around the room, taking note of

Martin's ill use of space and opportunity. "Man, if I had this room, there'd be a different bitch in here every night!"

Martin frowned in annoyance. "Do I need to remind you that this is a Christian college? Any guy caught on the girl's side, and vice-versa, spends the night in jail and is kicked off campus the next day. I don't want to go through that, and I sure wouldn't ask Hailey to risk that for me."

Martin and Hailey had been together since the seventh grade. When it was time to go to college, it was she who had decided upon the school, hoping that attending a Christian school together would alleviate the chance that new experiences and temptations that would drive a wedge between them. She had also decided that they were to get married upon graduation, and that he would work as a college professor, and she would teach courses online, which would give her plenty of time at home with their three future children.

"You need to learn how to do shit," Kareem chimed in. "You got this nice, corner room, with no other room joined to it. You can fuck all you want, and you don't even have to turn up your radio to drown out the sound. Me and Ahmil need this shit you got here, 'cause you ain't using her right!"

"I bet you and Ahmil would take full advantage ... every night," Martin joked, insinuating that the two would be with each other. They had picked up what he meant by the rise of his thick eyebrow and the sly grin that slashed his face.

"Fuck you, nigguh, and fuck that gay shit!" Kareem laughed, throwing his pillow on the carpeted floor to claim his crashing spot. He stretched his blanket into a rectangle and threw it on the floor along with the pillow. His sweaty body was lowered down next, each tight muscle in it gleaming beneath the florescent light.

Ahmil mimicked Kareem's ritual a few feet away, fixing his bed so that he and Kareem were foot-to-foot, leaving plenty of walk space for Martin to get to the bathroom during the night without tripping over them. "Every time we see this nigguh, he's talking about some ole fruity-tootie, dick in the bootie type shit," he laughed.

Oh God! Was he right? Martin tried to think back over the past conversations they had shared: their favorite Dragon ball-z episodes, weight training, Freestyle Friday on their favorite video show, 106&park, the best head they had ever gotten from a girl. Nope. He couldn't recall talking about any blatantly gay shit recently. Thank God! The dream really was beginning to screw with his head.

"I don't always talk about gay shit. You're full of shit!" he thought aloud. He regretted his words as soon as they tumbled free, overly defensive. Deep down, he knew that Ahmil and Kareem had only been joking. Now they would wonder why he was so serious all of a sudden, and all he wanted to do was drop the conversation. "When have I ever said anything gay?" he challenged, ignoring the voice of reason in his head, which begged him to shut the hell up and let the topic die.

An evil smirk crept over Ahmil's golden brown face. He and Kareem had Martin worked up now, and it was always fun to watch somebody who was usually so well-mannered utterly lose their composure. "Know how I know this nigguh is gay?" He nudged Kareem with his white-socked foot and motioned towards Martin. "Everything he eats has to be shaped like a dick: hotdogs and sausages. Tell the truth; that's all you've ever seen him eat, right? That's all I've ever seen him eat."

"You're fucking retarded!" Kareem literally doubled over with laughter. "Where did you come up with that one?"

"I'm gay because I ate a hotdog?" Martin was seconds away from throwing a full on tantrum. He wished that he had half the muscle that Kareem's mannish body possessed. He would have even settled for the wiry basketball player's physique of Ahmil over his own skinny, boyish body at that moment. He certainly wouldn't be the butt of all there jokes if he wasn't the runt. "That's all that's ever any good in the cafeteria!" Martin realized that he finally had the upper hand, and his demeanor calmed a bit. This was his room, not the public cafeteria and not Kareem's supped-up convertible. The cards were finally all in his hand. "If you keep up with this gay shit, you can take your sweaty ass right back to your own room, Ahmil. That goes for you, too, Kareem."

"Know how I know this nigguh gay?" Kareem couldn't resist. "Cause he's always on his damn period! This nigguh fusses more than my mom. And, come to think of it, he's more of a neat-freak. Make sure your blanket don't leave any lint on his floor, or we'll never finish hearing about that shit!"

"That's it!" Martin huffed, heading toward the door. "Kareem, grab your shit!"

"Know how else I know this nigguh gay," Kareem continued, completely ignoring Martin and the swinging door. "He wants to kick me out, so it's just you and him."

"Go on with that shit, Kareem!" Ahmil warned. "This air conditioner feels too good. I ain't laughing at nothing else you got to say tonight!"

Martin cleared his throat and motioned toward the door. "I mean it Kareem!"

"No you don't!" Kareem teased, fidgeting around in his pillow case. He pulled out a toothbrush holder and opened it to reveal a fat marijuana blunt. "Because if I go, this goes with me."

Martin hesitated at the open door, and then closed it. "I'm dead serious!" he warned, bending to jab a folded towel over the crack at the bottom of the door.

"I know," Kareem sighed, "And that's your whole problem. You're too damn serious. Why are you getting so upset, knowing that we always play like this? Now, it's Friday, we ain't got class tomorrow, your girl has one of the prettiest faces and fattest assess on campus, and she only has eyes for you. What you got to feel so salty about?"

"I don't want to talk about it, and that's it!" Martin breathed. The other guys knew him well enough to not press. They didn't have to. The whole story would tumble from his lips at any moment. All they had to do is wait him out and keep him talking.

"Fair enough," Ahmil smiled. "Say, didn't we leave a bottle of Hennessey in here a few weeks back?"

"Oh no you don't!" Martin snapped. "You guys will not come in here and turn my room into a frat house. I said you can sleep in here ... for the night!"

"You got something better to do than have a few shots with your boys?" Ahmil teased. "Tomorrow is Saturday." Ahmil knew that liquor made the task of keeping a secret more impossible for Martin, and he was dying to find out what had the usually well-composed boy on pins and needles.

Martin looked at the clock on his nightstand. It read 1:23 am. "Correction: today is Saturday!" He slid his closet door open a slit and squatted, sticking his hand into the darkness, unknowingly giving Kareem another view of his track star buns as he groped around for the bottle.

Kareem adjusted his hardening eight inches, and pulled the blanket over himself to aid in hiding his shame.

Martin spun around with the nearly full bottle of liquor. "I haven't touched her since the last time because I figured we should finish what we started together."

"That's what's up!" Ahmil smiled. "That's what I like about us. We don't make no moves behind one another's backs. I won't front; I'm closer with you two fools than I ever been with a lot of my boys back home, and I grew up with them."

"To us!" Martin smiled, holding the bottle towards heaven. He lowered it to his head and took three hard gulps before he felt the fire of the liquid course through his throat and chest. With a pitiful cough, he passed the bottle to Kareem, who now sat Indian style, the blanket still shielding his loins.

"Wait ... wait ... wait!" Ahmil protested before Kareem could tilt the huge bottle to his juicy lips. "We should finish everything we started, since we're all here together. We was playing this game: never ever-something."

"Never ever have I ever," Martin corrected. "Do we really want to get back into that?" During the last game, he had drunkenly revealed intimate details about his and Hailey's personal life. He had also learned things about his two friends that he wished he didn't know.

The objective of the game was for one person to stand and say something that they had never ever done ... or something that they would never ever do in a million years. Anybody present who had done this taboo thing had to take a drink. Being slightly older, Kareem had experienced a lot more than Ahmil and Martin, which is why they had him to thank for most of the emptiness that the bottle contained. They never did understand why Kareem chose to hang around with two freshmen when he was a second-year senior.

"I'll start," Ahmil insisted. "You can continue to hold the bottle Kareem. I know you going to have to drink to this one anyway."

"Come on with it!" Kareem laughed.

"Never ever have I ever stuck my finger up my own ass while I jacked off," Ahmil was so tickled that he could barely get the words out.

Kareem proudly took a gulp, and then looked around and said, "Who else going to be brave enough to tell the truth? I know you both have done that shit, too!" he offered the bottle to Martin, who had decided that he wasn't drinking to anything remotely gay, whether he had done it or not. The drink was waved away. "Well, I guess that means it's my turn." Kareem laughed. He tried to think of something that would be on their level. His erection had long subsided, allowing him the privilege of standing shameless in his tight, black briefs and saying, "Never ever have I ever ... um ... hmmm ... I don't know ... tasted my own cum when I jacked off." He handed the bottle to Ahmil before giving the boy proper time to process his words.

"I was only like twelve," Ahmil explained. "Fuck it, I'll drink to that," he drawled, reaching for the bottle.

Kareem pushed his hand away and took a gulp before passing the libation. He flashed the boys his shameless smile.

"Ewww! What would even make you guys want to taste your own spooge?" Martin frowned. That was one thing he had honestly never thought of doing.

"Okay ... .Oaky ... okay!" Ahmil grimaced, struggling to keep the focus on the game. He was one shot away from vomiting, and whether or not he took that shot was up to him, but he was far too stupid and too drunk to process that fact. "Never ever have I ever got head from a dope fiend." He turned the bottle up to his head and gulped before offering it around to Kareem and Martin.

"Get tested now!" Kareem laughed, pushing the bottle away. "You really let a crack head suck your dick, son?"

"Best damn head I ever got in my life!" Ahmil was now flat on his back, fighting to get his stomach to hold its burning contents.

"He's out of it," Kareem laughed, motioning toward Ahmil, who was slowly drawing himself into fetal position. "It's you and me now, Marty. Hmmm. Let me think of a good one." He reached over and took the bottle from Ahmil.

"No. It's my turn," Martin swallowed. The majority of his mind tried to talk him out of what he was about to disclose, but he couldn't fight against the tiny part that told him that his boys would see him through anything. "You're going to need to light the blunt for this one," he warned.

"It's major like that ... for real?" Kareem sat the bottle on the floor and turned over to retrieve the blunt from its tangle of blankets and sheets. Martin turned his head away in shame, trying to ignore the fact that one of Kareem's beige cheeks was visible as his briefs twisted sideways because of his odd positioning.

Goddamn! Why had that sight made Martin's dick stir in his own underwear?

"I got her," Kareem smiled, holding up the crinkled blunt. "So, what is it?"

"Promise me that you'll be honest with me!" Martin begged. "You admitted to all other kinds of shit. If you've ever done this, please don't bullshit me." Martin took the blunt from Kareem and breathed life into it with a flick of his orange lighter.

"What?" Kareem leaned forward and eagerly handed Martin the bottle. "I swear, if I did it, I'll admit that I did. Pinky swear."

"Pinky swear? That's pretty gay!" Ahmil's laugh came bubbling from the pile on the floor.

As gay as pinky swearing may have seemed, it provided Martin with some degree of confidence. He leaned in and offered Kareem his long, brown pinky. "Here goes," he muttered, picking the bottle up. "Never ever have I ever ..." He hesitated and drew in a breath, "dreamed about another man."

"What do you mean by dream?" Kareem asked, not wanting the answer to be the obvious.

"Have you ever dreamed that you were boning another dude?" Martin asked. Kareem watched as Martin's eyes glazed over with moisture. He could tell that the question wasn't based on a hypothetical situation.

Ahmil wasn't able to see the fear and desperation on Martin's face, or he wouldn't have yelled, "That nigguh is gay!" from his heap on the floor.

"Shut the fuck up!" Kareem warned, giving Ahmil's leg a less than gentle nudge with his foot. "No, Marty. That's not true at all. This happens to lots of perfectly heterosexual guys."

"But never you?" Martin swallowed. "I knew it. This is fucked! I knew I shouldn't have said anything."

"No! Wait!" Kareem called as Martin frantically pulled on his shorts and shoes. The last thing he needed was to have the poor bastard wandering around in his present state. He and Ahmil were certainly in no shape to chase after him. "You're the straightest guy I know, Marty! A dream is nothing but that ... a goddamn dream. You can't control what you dream about?"

"But you don't get it! It's not like I woke up, and I was disgusted with the dream. I wanted it to go on ... possibly forever. It felt so good to me, Kareem. Jesus, what's wrong with me?"

"Ain't shit wrong with you!" Kareem pulled Martin closer, until their bare torsos kissed. He cupped the crying boy's clean shaven head in his huge hands and whispered, "I got a secret for you, too."

Ahmil stirred from the floor. "It better not be what I think it is!" he slurred.

Kareem stood, frozen in confusion, his glassy green eyes focused on the torment on Martin's face, and then on Ahmil's angry, demanding stare. "Come on, Milli; we got to tell him," he pleaded with Ahmil.

"Tell me what?" Martin's curiosity was peeked now.

"A couple of months ago," Kareem began. He glanced over at Ahmil, who still shot him eyes that begged his silence. "Me and Ahmil did some things."

"Things?" Martin questioned. "What kind of things?"

"Shit. This is hard to explain," Kareem breathed. "What did you do with that blunt? I'm going to need it."

"What kind of things?" Martin demanded, handing over the lighter and the burned out blunt.

"Okay, this is what happened," Kareem sighed, sucking smoke into his lungs. He paused again, trying to hold the pungent substance long enough to feel the effect.

"You can stop this shit at any time," Ahmil tried to reason.

"Okay," Kareem breathed again. "You remember the freak test that was circulating through the emails a while back? The one that asked what you have and haven't done, sexually, and what you are willing to try?"

"Yeah. I deleted that shit." Martin nodded. "What about it?"

"Well, me and Milli took it, and our scores were nearly the same. Anyway, I let him see mine, and he let me see his, and it turns out that the one thing that neither of us had done was make out with a dude. It also turned out that both of us were ... well ... open-minded about the possibility."

"Wait!" Martin's heart beat fast, and his mouth went dry as he processed what his friend was about to tell him. "You guys did it?"

"Fuck no!" Ahmil interjected. "We didn't do shit. Nothing happened. That's why I don't understand why he's talking about this silly shit."

"Oh, something happened," Martin smiled, taking the blunt from Kareem, "Something that you don't want him to tell me about."

"Well, technically, he's telling you the truth; nothing happened," Kareem agreed, "but it almost did. We were smoking together and watching a flick, and I noticed Milli watching me from the side of his eye."

"That's some bullshit!" Ahmil interrupted. "If you got to talk about this shit, at least tell the truth. You were the one looking at my dick! You reached over and you grabbed my dick first! Before I had a chance to knock the hell out of you, it started feeling good. I was high ... and drunk."

"True," Kareem agreed. "I made the first move, 'cause you was on some ole peek-a-boo type shit, and I knew that a closed mouth don't get fed. But, when I did, you grabbed my dick right back, and when I kissed you, you kissed me right back. There's only one thing I did to you that night that you didn't do back to me, Milli! And you were not that drunk. You and I shared a six-pack. We usually go through twice that, and you're still able to drive. You just wanted to try some shit; admit it!"

"I knew you were going to find a way to work that part in about the one thing I didn't do back to you," Ahmil drunkenly chuckled. "I told you, nigguh, let it go! I couldn't do it. It just didn't feel right. It did at first, but then it was like something was wrong."

"Or maybe someone was missing," Kareem suggested, motioning towards Martin. "Maybe it wasn't meant to only be between you and me, Milli. Maybe it didn't feel right because Marty wasn't there with us."

"Whoa ... Whoa!" Martin laughed, passing the half-smoked blunt to Ahmil. "I had a dream about some dude that I had never even seen before. This shit that you talking is way different. I mean, even if it does turn out that I like dick, it may not be such a good idea to get it from the homies."

"Come on, guys!" Kareem tried to reason. "We all are interested in this shit. Why should we have to go find some random dudes to try the shit with when we're all right here right now? Think about it: we all know that we can trust each other. This shit will never leave this room. I don't know about you, two, but whether I actually like the shit or not, I would much rather say that I tried it with somebody that I care about."

"I guess he makes some good points," Ahmil breathed, releasing a thick cloud of smoke. "Ever since that thing almost happened with me and Kareem, I've been checking for dudes that may be down to try some shit. I figured that it may not be as weird with a stranger,

43

but every dude that I know will be down is so feminine and out there that I worry that they may try to call me out, or they're just not attractive. One thing I can say about all three of us is that we do look good."

"This is too surreal!" Martin laughed, clutching his head in his hands. "Not only are you both trying to talk me into some gay shit, but Ahmil, the pussy hound, Mr. 'I don't have one gay bone in my body,' is commenting on how good two guys look."

"Marty, all we're asking you to do is think about it," Kareem sighed.

A period of thirty second silence fell upon the room before Martin broke it with, "Okay. So, say that I do agree to it, how would we start?"

"Well," Kareem swallowed, "I guess the first thing is for all three of us to agree that this is something that we all want to try. It's not just the weed or the liquor. We have to get that out of the way right now, so that things won't get weird for us later."

"Agreed," Martin said. "If we do this, it's not going to be blamed on the alcohol."

"Fair enough," Ahmil agreed, "but the second rule is that it stays between the three of us ... forever!"

Martin's eyes scanned his two friends, taking in the beauty of their sweat glistening skin, Ahmil's skinny, boyish, butterscotch form, covered in thin, silky patches of curly hair, and Kareem's smooth, hairless, beige skin stretched over the tight, protruding muscles of his thick but slender torso. He imagined kissing Kareem's pouty, pink lips, and of running his hands through his curly afro as he stared into his sleepy, bedroom eyes. He imagined seeing the two lumps that he had been watching in the back of Ahmil's underwear, thanks to his friend's preference to baggy, sagging jeans, in its full glory. He imagined running his hands over Ahmil's skinny body, and of kissing him while his fingers tangled in the boy's frizzy cornrows. "I agree," he nervously sighed. "Nothing that we do here goes beyond us three. So, what do we do now?"

Kareem stood and slowly etched his bikini briefs down, revealing his semi-erect eight inches. "We can start with just head," he suggested.

"I knew that's what you were going to say," Ahmil laughed. "You've been trying to get me to do that shit for nearly a month now, and the answer is still no!"

"Well, I'm down." Martin shrugged. "But I don't just do you; you do me back."

"You know I got you." Kareem smiled, walking over to Martin. He waved the thick, uncut muscle before the boy's face, and Martin hesitantly opened his mouth, accepting a bit more than he could handle. He released it with a cough, but the taste and the feel of his mouth being invaded was more pleasurable than he cared to admit. He was back on the growing lump of veins in a matter of seconds, allowing Kareem to pump in and out of the back of his throat. He was so turned on that he rose up in his chair and freed his own throbbing nine inches from the confines of his basketball shorts.

"Yawl are really doing this shit!" Ahmil watched, awe-stricken, from his place on the floor, less than five feet away from the action. His own thick cock strained against his mesh boxers. Nervously, he crawled over to his friends and pulled himself into a standing position. Resting with one arm around Kareem to help with his balance, he pulled the front of his boxers down and allowed his seven and a half inches to tumble free, the slit in the head already glistening with moisture. "You might as well suck this, too," he offered, sliding his dick across Martin's cheek. Martin spat out Kareem's spit-covered dick and turned to take Ahmil's into his mouth.

Kareem lowered himself to his knees and pushed Martin's hand away from his own throbbing dick. He took the thick, curved nine inches into his hands and pumped, enjoying the heaviness, and waved it back and forth. "Damn, Hailey is getting all of this? No wonder she's always in a good mood," he joked, and then he dove in for the kill, sucking over half of it into his mouth. When he tried to go past the curve in the center, he choked, and realized that he had better work on the tip and the large, mushroom head instead of deep-throating. Martin moaned his approval of what Kareem was doing, and Ahmil echoed similar sentiment, pushing in and out of Martin's wet mouth.

"Don't stop it; nigguh, don't stop!" Ahmil moaned, caressing Martin's bald head.

Kareem jerked around at the sound of Ahmil's deep moans, and his eyes locked on the boy's butterscotch ass cheeks, flexing as they forced his engorged cock in and out of Martin's slobbering mouth. Kareem's hands followed his eyes, landing on the glistening mounds of flesh, and causing Ahmil to tense up. He slowly ran his index finger down the length of the boy's slit, stopping to attempt pressing it into his tight hole.

"Come on, Kareem," Ahmil sighed, pushing his hand away. "Why you always got to make shit feel weird?"

"Fuck that shy, virgin shit tonight!" Kareem protested, placing his hand back. "We agreed that we going to get ten types of freaky in this bitch, and that's what I plan on doing. Besides, more than just my fingers is going up in that ass, so you better be glad I'm trying to get you prepared."

"I think you a faggot for real," Ahmil sighed, and tried his best to ignore Kareem's probing fingers and lavish the feeling he was getting from Martin, who now sat stroking his own dick with a feverish intensity.

"Enough of this blowjob shit," Kareem sighed, pulling Ahmil away from Martin, whose mouth made a sound like popping gum as Ahmil's dick tumbled free from his lips. "Bend over this chair," he demanded of Ahmil, who stared at him like a deer in headlights. "Trust me!" he insisted. "You know I won't do shit to hurt you, boy!"

Too drunk to protest or support himself without help any longer, Ahmil threw his slinky torso over the back of the chair, lending his ass upward to whatever Kareem had in mind. His breathing returned to normal when Kareem squatted behind him, tracing his crack with the tip of his tongue. After a few seconds, that grew into him deeply probing the boy's hole with the slick serpent of a tongue, snaking his way in and out of his cavity as Ahmil gripped the chair and moaned in drunken discomfort.

"I wanna try that shit, too," Martin drawled, leaving his chair to crawl behind Kareem and lick his already exposed hole.

"Do it right!" Kareem spat out Ahmil's rim long enough to demand. "Get my shit gushy wet!"

"I'm a eat this lil yellow ass out like some pussy!" Martin promised, spreading the cheeks wide with his fingers. He spat in the exposed, twitching hole, and then lapped at the puddle as it dripped down the winking rosebud. He used the tip of his tongue to push some of the saliva into the shuttering hole. All the while he could hear Ahmil's whimpers and moans above his head. He wasn't so sure that Ahmil was as pleased to have a tongue in his ass as Kareem, but he was certain that Kareem was enjoying everything he was doing. The man was throwing his skinny ass backwards, almost smothering Martin in attempts to make Martins tongue dig further in his crease.

Just when Martin had fully committed himself to the task of licking the hole and keeping his balance against Kareem's wild bucking, Kareem stood from his job of sucking Ahmil's rim. He spun around so fast that his hard cock slapped Martin in the face. He seized Martin by the shoulders and pulled the boy into a standing position. The tongue that he had just retrieved from Ahmil's cavity was crammed into Martin's mouth, and Martin accepted it, suckling it as if it were the sweetest thing that he had ever tasted. Their crotches mingled as they kissed, smearing pre-cum all over one another's stomachs, thighs and dicks.

"AWWWW ... MMMMMMM," They could still hear Ahmil moan, so drunk that he couldn't remove himself from the chair.

"Let me eat this little ass," Kareem begged, reaching behind Martin and popping his cheeks so hard that they jiggled. "Bend over this chair," he instructed pulling another chair beside the one Ahmil lay crouched over.

"You're a real freak." Martin obeyed, pushing the chair over closer to Ahmil's. He didn't want his friend left out of another moment of the ordeal. They had agreed that it would be the three of them through it all. He leaned himself over and kissed Ahmil's pouty, pink lips, and then his closed eyelids. His hands began to walk up and down the boy's torso as he felt Kareem's long tongue invade his own welcoming ass. His fingers crept down Ahmil's back and found the slick spot between his cheeks, the spot that Kareem's lavish tongue had just abandoned. The hole was still shuttering in and out, leaking with Kareem's saliva, just wet enough to allow Martin to push his middle finger in.

"Fuck!" Ahmil groaned, and his back arched. His bloodshot eyes flew open and landed, questioningly on Martin's smiling face.

"Just making sure you're still with us," Martin teased, slowing the pace of his probing finger down inside of Ahmil to match the rhythm that Kareem's fingers and tongue played inside his own spread canyon. He didn't know if Ahmil was enjoying the feel of his hole being invaded as much as he was enjoying the sensation of what Kareem's long tongue and two thick fingers were

49

doing inside of him, but he certainly was enjoying the feel of the boy's tight opening contracting around his wiggling finger. He decided not to stop, despite the boy's pitiful moaning.

"This shit is crazy!" Ahmil squirmed, reaching to grab Martin's fully erect nine inches. He rolled the swollen head around in his fingertips, too drunk to keep any special rhythm. Martin still moaned his approval of his friend's soft touch.

Martin leaned over again, tracing the outline of Ahmil's thick lips with the tip of his tongue. To his surprise, his friend opened his mouth this time, accepting the tongue into his warm mouth. The sound of their lips pressing together began to compete with the perpetual smacking sound that Kareem's mouth made around Martin's rim, and with the gushing noise that Ahmil's rim made as Martin's finger dove in and out. They were so entangled in their sweet kiss that it took them a few seconds to notice that Kareem had abandoned them to rummage for condoms in Martin's drawers.

They were still kissing when he returned, condoms and Vaseline in hand. "Which one to go with first?" Kareem marveled, looking at the two asses offered up to his perversion. "Milk chocolate?" He slapped Martin's ass so hard that the boy' back arched on impulse. "Or butterscotch?" Ahmil let out a yelp as Kareem's hand crashed down hard on his humble cheeks.

"Whatever you do to us, we get to do back to you!" Martin reminded, looking over his shoulder. It all still seemed surreal to him as he watched Kareem pull a rubber over his erection. Only the burning sensation of his rim, where Kareem's tongue and two fingers had just abandoned, told him that he wasn't still dreaming.

"I think butterscotch got a little more bounce to it," Kareem beamed, lining his condomed dick head up with Ahmil's entrance.

Martin wasn't sure whether to be disappointed or grateful that he wasn't picked first. Either way, he leaned over again, kissing Ahmil, and rubbing his back to take his mind off of what was sure to be a painful entry, as Kareem's eight inches were beer-can-thick.

"AHHHH ... AWWW ... .Shit!!!" Ahmil yelped beneath his breath as more and more of Kareem's dick was pushed into his stretched opening. He closed his eyes and wrapped his fingers tight around the back of the chair to aid in taking the pain.

"You can take it!" Kareem coaxed, jabbing in and out of the boy, who clearly was not ready. "Don't run from it. Just let me get that ass."

"Get it!" Ahmil whimpered. "I'm a soldier, nigguh; I ain't running. Take it like you want it."

"That's my boy!" Kareem smiled, wrenching deeper. He slowed down only to reach over and work two fingers inside or Martin's welcoming ass. All the while, Martin cooed in Ahmil's ear and laced the boy's face with kisses, begging him to be strong and take what Kareem was doing to him. His tactics seemed to be working. Soon Ahmil was so into the ordeal that he was throwing his ass backwards to meet Kareem's thrust, making his cheeks crash against Kareem's muscular thighs with such an impact that it sounded as if somebody was being slapped over and over again.

Martin was glad that his room was at the end of the hall instead of joined on to another room like every other room on the hall. The last thing he needed was for people to hear the moaning that Ahmil was doing, especially when it grew into a warrior's chant of "I'm a take this dick, nigguh! This shit hurt, but I'm taking it!"

Kareem laughed and removed himself from Ahmil's tight opening, watching as the hole worked in and out, trying to push itself back in place. He wiped sweat from his brow and gave Ahmil's reddening ass cheeks another slap with his hand, and then he walked behind Martin and began spanking the boy's cheeks with his still hard dick. "You going to be a soldier, too?" he teased. "Ahmil is the baby of the group, too, nigguh. You better not let me find out that he can handle the dick better than you can."

"Go on put it in," Martin teased back, cockily. "Just remember, anything you do to me, I get to do right back to you; so don't get in this ass and start bucking like you lost your damn mind!"

"Ain't nobody trynna hurt you," Kareem promised, pressing his thick tip into the flexing hole.

Martin bit down on the leather backing of the chair to prevent the building scream from escaping his throat. Soon, the painful entry was over and Kareem was stirring his guts up like mashed potatoes, rocking in and out of the boy's channel so fast that the chair bucked beneath him, threatening to fall over. Martin freed himself from the fear of toppling over by taking his long legs from being wrapped around the chair and putting his feet on the floor. His shoulders and chest remained flat on the chair, but his ass was poked further up, making it easier for Kareem to slam in and out of his tunnel.

"How does that shit feel?" Kareem teased. "You like this big dick up in your guts, boy?"

"Hell yeah!" Martin lied, not wanting to be upstaged by how well Ahmil had taken the intrusion. "Gimme that entire yellow dick! I can take it!"

"That's what I wanted to hear," Kareem smiled, withdrawing from the tight opening. "I got the whiskey dick tonight; it's going to be a while before I bust, and I know neither of yawl trying to fuck with this big snake for that long," he explained, giving Martin's questioning face a gentle kiss. "Let me watch you fuck Ahmil."

"I don't know about all that; Milli looks like he's really out of it," Martin appraised watching as Ahmil still whimpered and humped up and down in his chair. He wasn't sure, but he was almost certain that he saw tears forming in the poor kid's eyes.

"Fuck that shit!" Ahmil protested. "I'm down for my mother fucking nigguhs. I don't care how bad it hurt; I'm taking the dick tonight!"

"You heard'im," Kareem laughed handing Martin a rubber and the jar of baby powder scented Vaseline. "Still, go a little easy on'im. You know he's a crybaby underneath all this thug shit he talks."

"One last chance to change your mind!" Martin warned, lining his pulsing head up with Ahmil's swollen entrance.

"Nigguh, I said fuck me," Ahmil demanded.

Martin pushed in and Ahmil let out a yelp and punched the chair in pain. "I don't even want to do this shit," Martin whispered to him. "The ass feels good and all, but if you tell me to stop, I will. You don't got to prove shit to us, nigguh. I know you a G!"

"I'm taking it ... .all of it!" Ahmil insisted, pushing himself further back on the chair so that his ass stuck out to meet Martin's long, deep strokes. "Fuck me like you want this ass, too, nigguh! Put some stank on it!"

"Oh, you getting cocky?" Martin teased wrenching wildly into the boy's opening. "This how you want me to fuck you? You want me to treat you like you my bitch?"

"AWWW!!! No! No!" Ahmil grimaced. "I was talking all that shit, but I can't take it. Slow down."

"Damn right!" Martin laughed. "So from now on, just lay there and take this dick the way I'm giving it to your little drunk ass!"

"Alright, Daddy," Ahmil promised. "You can get it how you want it ... just be easy!"

"Oh shit; that nigguh just called you Daddy!" Kareem laughed. "Let me find out the dick is really that good."

"Oh, you will!" Martin promised, still wrenching in and out of Ahmil. He leaned forward and stuck out his tongue, hoping that if they kissed, it would silence the annoying whimpering sounds that Ahmil was making. It was to no avail. The sounds seemed to get even worse. As good as Ahmil's tightness felt to him, he couldn't put up with hearing his friend sound like he was in so much pain. He withdrew and snatched the rubber off, giving Ahmil's ass cheeks one more smack with his hands. "You're a big thug-baby, you know that?" he laughed. He then turned to Kareem and said, "Now let's see how you can handle the dick!"

"Oh, I can take some pain; I been shot before, and I been stabbed twice!" Kareem laughed, showing off the scars that he was always so proud of. "The only problem is that yawl need to decide who's gonna fuck me, cause there is only one rubber left."

"Bullshit!" Martin protested. "You fucked the hell out of both of us. We said nobody does anything to anybody that doesn't get done back to them! We said that; remember!"

"I'm down to take a dick ... just flip a coin!" Kareem laughed.

"Fuck flipping a coin!" Martin fumed. "It's my room, and it's my rubber, so it's my ass. Bring it on over here!"

"Bullshit!" Ahmil thundered, finally able to leave the chair. His legs were wobbly as he padded across the floor to address Martin, and he wondered if it was from all of the dick he'd taken or the alcohol. "Both of yawl nigguhs just banged my guts out! I probably won't be able to shit for weeks, and you telling me I don't get to fuck nobody? Yawl nigguhs ain't going to bitch me out! If I don't get no cutty, I'm fitting to body somebody; so one of yawl needs to bend the fuck over!"

"That's why I love this kid!" Kareem doubled over with laughter. "Arm wrestle for the ass."

"No!" Martin insisted. "This time Ahmil just got to stop playing the baby role. It's my turn to fuck! Besides, this nigguh can't even stand up; what he going to do with some ass?"

"Fuck you!" Ahmil wailed as a push from Martin caused him to go crashing to the floor. "I'm drunk tonight, but tomorrow, you can get fucked up!"

"Look; it ain't going to be all of that!" Kareem reprimanded, stepping between the two of them. "Both of yawl want it, both of yawl can get it."

"I don't go raw!" Martin frowned.

"Nobody said you had to. Follow my directions and see what I teach you." Kareem smiled. "Lay on your back, the opposite way Ahmil is laying. Now scoot down until yawl balls is touching."

"What?" Ahmil laughed. "That's some real gay shit you talking. I don't want his balls on mine."

"Do it!" Kareem insisted. Martin obeyed with a shrug, and watched, awestricken, as Kareem forced both he and Ahmil's cocks together into a bouquet. The condom was then stretched over both heads and meticulously etched down until it covered the base of both cocks.

"I know this nigguh ain't going to try to do what I think!" Martin shuddered.

Kareem expelled his disbelief as he squatted over the double-headed beast he had just created and fingered an ample supply of Vaseline into his tight hole. "I'm going to take both yawl nigguhs' down to the base on the count of three," he promised, pushing his rim against their heads. "One ... .two ... three!" With a painful jab, he had worked both penises inside of him, and sat fighting back tears as the boys kept perfectly still beneath him, giving him a chance to regain his composure.

"I know this shit hurt," Ahmil sighed. "One dick at a time felt like I was being ripped in two."

"I'm a real G, though, Nigguh!" Kareem moaned. "When you become a big boy, maybe you can take pain, too!"

"That's how we know this nigguh really is gay," Martin couldn't help but joke. "He is taking two big black dicks like one of them white bitches from Dogfart.com!"

Kareem bore his weight on Amil's bent knee and rode both dicks feverishly as he whacked away at his own swollen dick with his greasy palm. "Yawl better stop trying to get jokes in and get a nut, cause once I bust, this shit is over!" he warned. "And I'm almost there!"

"Oh fuck!" Ahmil hissed in discomfort as he felt Martin's penis slide against his, glazing him with pre-cum.

"I'm cumin'!" Martin announced, so turned on by the sure extremeness of it all that he couldn't help but to release all over Ahmil's pulsing cock.

"I'm coming, too!" Kareem announced, but he still rode like a mad man, as Ahmil hissed from the sensation of Martin's fluids being rubbed into his sensitive skin. Kareem's sperm flew out in abundance, and he pumped and rode like a maniac, sending most of it flying unto Martin's face and chest. Some landed on Ahmil's thighs. "Go on and bust, too, Milli!" he coaxed, "Shoot that shit for me!"

Ahmil turned nearly as red as Kareem had become during the whole ordeal and began to flay around like a fish out of water. His drunken legs peddled up and down, like he was riding an imaginary bike, and he bit down on his tongue to hold in a scream as his cream burst forward, mixing with the mess Martin had already made of the condom, and bubbling down the bases of both he and Martin's still hard cocks.

"Goddamn! That's what I'm talking about!" Kareem cheered, hopping up from his seat of cocks and ripping the condom from the boys' dicks. He knelt like a dog and began to lap the white grossness away from their soppy cocks as they moaned with sensitivity. When he had devoured every drop, he joined his friends on the floor, all three breathing piquantly.

"Well boys." Martin sighed. "We did it. And it doesn't go any further than this room."

58

"Why you keep saying that it doesn't leave this room?" Ahmil laughed. "We know that it stays between us. Who would we even want to know this shit?"

"You want to know why he keeps saying it, Milli?" Kareem laughed. "It's because Marty is a closet faggot. As long as nobody knows what he does, it's all good with him."

"Ha ha, mother fucker!" Martin snickered. "Well what does it make you, Mr. I can take two dicks at once?"

"Know how I know Kareem's gay, Martin?" Ahmil laughed. "Cause he gave me and you these little homo pet names: Marty and Milli."

"Know how I know both of yawl gay?" Kareem retaliated. "Cause I can smell yawl booty get wet every time I call yawl that shit!"

All three cuddled together laughing, until Martin sat up with a serious look on his face. "Wait! We just fucked!" he groaned. "Exactly what does it mean if it doesn't mean we're faggots?"

"It means we got a nut together." Kareem shrugged. "You aren't going to get all mushy on us just 'cause we gave you some dick and some ass; are you?"

"No. you're right." Martin chuckled. "It was just some shit that happened ... once, between three good friends. And it doesn't leave this room."

"Nigguh, if you say that shit one more time, you won't leave this room," Ahmil laughed. "Now no more talking; let's just try to sleep."

"Agreed," Kareem insisted.

"Okay; agreed," Martin sighed, but even when the other boys' laughter had turned into snores, he lay there all night pondering what had just happened between the three of them.

COSPLAY
By Lawrence Jackson

Lawrence Jackson is a thirty-one-year old writer living in London, author of the erotic fantasy MISADVENTURE IN SPACE AND TIME. He'd love to hear from you on Twitter @misljackson

Adventure can strike anywhere – even at a sci-fi convention ...

It was cabaret hour at the Bovary Hotel, Bournemouth, and the Monsters were the first to take their seats.

Silver-fingers outstretched, the Cybermen pressed through the swing doors – a small gaggle of them were talking on the stairs. It takes a certain sort of man to become a Cyberman: a cyborg zombie from the coldest reaches of space, blank-faced and blank-souled, their emotions deprogrammed. The eye holes on one, set in a replica of the silver 1968 helmet, were so narrow its occupant needed some assistance, on account of the Axminster carpet. Arm in arm, the terrifying monsters sought out their little table and sat down.

Music was playing through the wall-mounted speakers. On an ordinary Saturday night in the ballroom, one might have heard "In the Mood" by Glenn Miller, perhaps even a wedding DJ's medley of '80s and '90s chart-toppers. Tonight the music was "All the Strange, Strange Creatures," a bit of orchestral incidental music that made even the hotel's cozy decor seem slightly otherworldly and dangerous.

Two scaly Silurians (one of them the great Madame Vastra) and a woman dressed, improbably, as a 1960s Police Telephone Box were next through the door, followed immediately by a squidgy-faced Zygon, another Cyberman, a woman dressed as Captain Jack, a man dressed as Leela, then more and further guests, laughing and chatting, shyly or garrulously, seeking out friends and bagging seats near the stage or the bar, depending on how they meant to spend their evening.

It was the first night of Enlightenment, a modestly sized UK convention for fans of *Doctor Who,* a TV series also known, by most of those gathered here beneath a spinning mirror ball, as the "Greatest TV Program Ever Made."

Of course, thought Alastair MacRae, not everyone was an alien. Some guests were too self-consciously "grown up" to take up the organizers' invitation to so-called "cosplay": they felt more dignified in M&S slacks and a plaid shirt. But besides them, the Monsters and the Companions were the Doctors: the hero of the show in all his incarnations: frock coats, tweed jackets, checked trousers, and inordinately long scarves. It was good to see – but it was harder to spot Andy in the crowd.

He ran his hand nervously over his freshly cropped hair, at the same time drumming on the table, trying to search the crowd without meeting any eye but the one he wanted. It wasn't that he was averse to conversation, but Andy was the reason he was there, after all. He had always felt a little like an alien in disguise until he had his son by his side.

"I must congratulate you on your costume," said a voice to his left. It was male and young, and he turned toward it with a smile, knowing almost immediately it wasn't the man he was waiting for.

"Thanks," he said politely, not given to talking a lot.

The stranger was older than Andy, but not by much – someone a few years out of University, rather than embarking upon it – fussily dressed and clean-shaven, with intelligent eyes and a wide smile. "I noticed you earlier. The only UNIT soldier in the house, and your uniform, I must say, is impeccable."

Alastair looked down at his khaki costume, as though he had not really seen it yet. In truth, he found it hard to meet the young man's eyes. In Alastair's experience, men didn't complement each other on their choice of outfit. Alastair rarely even noticed what his mates had on. In this context, of course, the remark was completely normal and flattering. It was about attention to detail, originality, and celebrating something bigger than either of them.

He was bigger than he used to be though. He had time to work out more often these days and was seeing decent gains. It was getting a bit tight around the chest and upper arms. It was a sign of how things changed and stayed the same. Would he ever wear it again? He was glad, at least, if it had done him proud this last time.

"More my era than yours, I think," he said, with a shy smile. "When I was a wee kid in the '70s, I thought the Brigadier was the star of the show."

"I'm pretty sure the Brigadier always thought so, too," said the other man. "But I have to tell you, you're wrong."

Alastair froze, preparing himself to be corrected on some small point of continuity. It always seemed to happen once an hour at these things.

The man's smile and eyes widened boyishly, though his voice was soft. "I absolutely love those stories."

Alastair laughed with relief. "Glad to hear it."

"It seems a happier time for the Doctor when his people exile him to Earth. He's not a solitary wanderer in space and time, he's got a family round him. The Brigadier, Captain Yates, even the evil Master ..."

"And don't forget Jo Grant," Alastair cut in. "Gorgeous young thing."

The young man wagged a finger. "Now, I don't think the Doctor had any interest in that sort of thing."

"I did! Particularly during ... oh, damn, what was it ... Alien planet. Ice caves."

"Planet of the Daleks," said the man, as though it were obvious. "Episode 3 has one of my all-time favorite cliffhangers."

"I was thinking more of Jo's skirt," Alastair said, "but you're right. I could never resist a good cliffhanger."

A hand settled on his shoulder, and he looked up. A familiar young man was standing behind him, grinning through a tangle of beard. "Dad! Sorry I kept you waiting, keep bumping into people from last year."

Al raised an eyebrow. "I can survive okay by myself, you know. I've been chatting to, uh ..."

"John," said the young man, lifting his drink in greeting. Alastair responded with a cheerful salute then turned back to his son. Strange to see him looking taller than ever, somehow – the black Edwardian outfit only seemed to accentuate it.

"You're dressed appropriately. We were just now talking about Jon Pertwee."

Andy frowned in confusion and glanced down at his costume. "Dad, this isn't Pertwee. It's Capaldi. Honestly, don't you watch the new series at all?"

Alastair's heart sank. "I may have missed some lately," he said. He didn't want to say in front of his new acquaintance that he felt less temptation to watch it without his son beside him on the sofa. And in the last year, he had discovered Saturday night was the best and quietest of all evenings to visit the gym.

John's bright voice lifted the mood suddenly. "Ah, they're not so very different looks," he said. "I think Peter Capaldi was definitely watching *Planet of the Daleks* back in 1973 with you, Al."

"Back when it was really good," Al said, buoyed up enough to be cheeky.

Andy rolled his eyes, but it was an affectionate gesture, and an adolescent one, despite the facial hair. "Anyway, the fun's starting any minute. You guys want a beer?"

John declined politely, his glass still half-full. He looked the kind of lightly-built man who might be bowled over by one drink too many. Alastair accepted, but awkwardly, offering to accompany him or lend him cash. As Andy disappeared into a crowd of extra-terrestrials, Alastair tried to explain to John.

"I'm still not used to him being of age to drink. Openly, with me, that is ... like any other guy. Forget I'm not responsible for him anymore."

"Isn't that good?"

"Oh, it's great, of course," he said quickly. "He's away on a great adventure. Plus, he hasn't passed his test yet, so I still get to drive him to places like this!"

"Yes, I thought it wasn't your scene," John said. "But I'm glad you're here."

"Oh, aye?"

"The entertainment your son mentioned – I'm not sure I want to see Bonnie Langford and Colin Baker duet on 'Star Trekkin'." He fiddled with his neckwear. "Not twice in one lifetime, anyway."

Alastair winced. Andy arrived back with two pints of locally brewed bitter. "Nice bow tie, by the way. You're one for the Second Doctor, then, I take it?"

The young man in the tweed jacket and red braces looked down at himself, back at Alastair, seemed about to contradict him, then think better of it. Alastair assumed he'd been due to be corrected on another point of continuity, but John had spared him. A glow of affection touched his heart. As the three of them clinked glasses, Alastair felt only slightly out of place, as if a member of a Masonic lodge had seen him fumble a secret handshake but admitted him anyway.

The lights dimmed, and the mirror ball clicked off, leaving the little galaxy of table lamps glowing and the big silver moon spotlight. The night was underway.

After a couple of pints and a comedy routine based around obscure items of *Doctor Who* merchandise – a routine at which Andy and John had laughed hard throughout, while Alastair forced a smile – the older man excused himself and went out for a smoke. He only partook in times of stress and then mainly for the law that required you to leave the crowd and go out in the cool, autumnal darkness.

Sure enough, the stress melted to a lukewarm sensation of melancholy. The taste of the tobacco tarnished the air, and his heart rate slowed. He could hear the sea nearby, and music from inside the hotel, and rumbles of applause. In his starchy soldier uniform, he felt like a man guarding the happy crowd within from some dangerous force out in the night. Then a man shuffled past dressed as what looked like a five-foot-nine penis in a green velvet cloak, and he remembered that it was all a fantasy – and Alastair had no duty to protect anyone or anything anymore.

As he watched the weird alien creature make its way carefully back into the hotel foyer, he saw John pass it, turning to give it a sceptical look. The electric light threw his handsome features into strange-looking shadows, but as he approached, his expression gave Alastair a renewed sense of solidarity at the absurdity of it all.

"What a dick," Alastair joked, gesturing after it with his fag packet.

"I'll have you know," said John, "that was an ambassador from Alpha Centauri. An excitable race, with six hands and no distinguishing sexual organs."

"You could have fooled me," said Alastair. "Where's that from, then?"

"*Curse of Peladon*, 1972, with your Jo Grant," John replied, declining a cigarette with a simple gesture, "And *Monster of Peladon*, 1974. *Symbolises Doctor Who* fandom, I always think: benevolent, excitable, slightly daft ..."

"No sex?"

John actually considered this seriously. "I wouldn't say that. But *Who* fandom has always had a queer character to it. Alpha Centauri doesn't have any conventional gender, but the Doctor is perfectly charming toward it."

"I can't believe you can remember the name of a character from a TV show made before you were born," said Alastair. "I don't remember it, and I was there!"

"I always remember the monsters," said John, wryly. "And you remember Jo Grant's short skirt from the planet Spiridon."

"That's different," said Alastair, drawing on his cigarette, and letting out a sigh of smoke. "That's sex. An awakening. I told you, she was gorgeous: petite, cute wee face framed in golden hair, and then the short skirts. Oh, delicious legs. I'd have been about ten years old, and I had an instant stoner every time I thought of her." He was beginning to feel the stirrings of one now, in the trousers of his UNIT uniform. The thought amused him, and he wondered if he could mention it to John without him getting the wrong idea.

"But, the Brigadier was still the star of the show."

"I never fancied him … not that way inclined. Plus he had that shitty fake stache."

John laughed at that, and Alastair, feeling encouraged, lit up a fresh ciggie. John refused again. Obviously he'd come out for Al's company, not a smoke. Alastair wondered if Andy would join them as well, and whether he would want that.

The vague thought crossed his mind that getting John to take a drag on a cigarette would be pleasing: that he was too good and deserved leading astray. He tucked his fag packet back in his trousers; it nudged against the semi in his trousers. For some reason, it refused to go quietly.

"Dinnae get me wrong," he said, abruptly. "About knowing who Alpha Whatsit is. I respect it. No, I love it. Like Andy and his costume, or you and your bow tie. Andy's Mum always looked at it askance. When we split, she made him leave all his DVDs and things at my place. She discouraged him from watching it."

"I didn't realize you were separated," John said. "I'm sorry."

"Oh, I'm used to it by now," he said, waving it away. "The important thing is she didn't see what it all meant. It means caring about something bigger than you. It means, not giving in to the cynics."

"Being in love, after everything."

"That's exactly what it is." He trod out his cigarette. "Ach, I sound soft. It's just, Andy going off to Uni … it's left me feeling a bit redundant."

"But like you say," said the man in the bow tie, "he treasures childlike things, like all this …" John waved his hands about abstractly. "You and him, that's not lost."

"It's changing, though." He looked down at his boots. "I'll have to change. Fifty years young and alone again. Could be a tricky maneuver." He forced a laugh, shook his head, drew cold night air through his teeth over a smoke-dried tongue.

The younger man was looking at him seriously. "The Doctor changed at least six times between 1963 and 1989. I know technically that's because they recast him: to me, though, he's just that sort of man."

"Ah, but he had the delectable Jo at his side when he was doing it. And a list of other fuckable girls before and after." He shrugged. "A man does need a companion."

John seemed to hesitate before speaking. "Or at least a monster."

"Most men would like a monster, I think," Alastair quipped, but neither of them were laughing. Alastair's dick was hardening again, slowly, like taking a long drag on his cigarette, and he didn't quite know why.

John let out a breath, betraying the fact he'd been holding it. "Yes," he said. "And some of us have them." He looked awkwardly down at his shoes.

Stop looking down, you'll see it, why am I hard, what does this mean?

"Dad?" Andy was suddenly there, leaning out of the hotel doorway, his smart suit looking like a stage magician's. "Thought you should know the torture is over."

71

"See you inside," Alastair called, his voice thick. The erection had melted at the sound of his son's voice, but still he felt something else: not the melancholy any more, and not the stress, but a tautness in his muscles, a tightness in his chest. Was it just that his uniform felt suddenly closer on him than ever? Like half-way into a work-out, his body woken up by the first set of reps but ready to be pushed much further.

He looked at John, and John met his gaze perfectly. Who was this man, anyway? All they'd been talking about, before his unexpected opening up, was Doctor bloody Who. What did this slightly effete young fellah do, beyond this hotel, outside Bournemouth, in the working week? He was nice – almost too nice, Alastair thought. He was lanky and slender, the red braces pressing his shirt to him crisply. He had the body of a *Doctor Who* fan – not an outdoors type, not sporty, somehow almost delicate. Alastair thought again how easily a man like this would get drunk and wanted to push him gently in that direction.

"Come on," he said, "I owe you a drink for listening to my woes. And you can tell me some more of yours, if you like."

"Fine," said John turning away. "I could never resist a good cliff-hanger."

But when they were inside, necking the local ale, jostled in with Andy and his pals beneath a stuffed, framed trout, the conversation inevitably ran in another direction. All about how this year's season was improving on last year's season, and how the seasons of thirty years ago were better by miles, untouchably good.

It was a conversation Alastair was used to, in the pub with his mates talking football: what needed to happen in the next transfer window, what went wrong last season, how Rangers could never match the Willie Johnston glory days of 1972. But Alastair knew who Willie Johnston was.

He managed to get the subject back to costumes: None of the Doctor Who's, he said, had ever looked as right as Jon Pertwee. He meant it partly as covert praise for his son's choice of outfit, remembering too late that Andy wasn't dressed as Pertwee, it was the new bloke. He was slightly pissed, he realized, and his mind was running wild. He kept looking across at John, talking animatedly to a woman in a coat loud enough to induce a migraine. John's long face, proud nose, strong jaw, wild hair – who was he, and what did he suddenly mean to Alastair?

At half eleven, the crowd began to shift. Andy patted his dad's cropped scalp to get his attention. They were all going to a midnight screening of the anniversary story. Was Al up for that?

"Ah," he said, "No, I think I'll get to bed. This modern era, it's not really me."

Andy smiled. "See you at the Katy Manning panel tomorrow, then?"

"Yeah, yeah, of course," replied Alastair, thinking Who? and making a beeline for the door. As he climbed the stairs, he felt someone put a hand on his arm and knew, with a strange thrill, who it would be.

"I was thinking, while they watch their modern stuff," John said, and Alastair felt the wire pulling tighter. "Well, I've got *Planet of the Daleks* on DVD."

A warm wave of relief swept over Alastair. There was nothing to worry about, after all. Just pals watching some daft sci-fi with pretty girls in. The perfect end, in fact, to a strange day.

John's hotel room was smaller than the twin room Alastair was in. After John set up the DVD player there was nowhere for them to sit but side-by-side on the single bed, backs on headboard, John's thigh hard against Alastair's. The body warmth between them was novel for Alastair, but to move his leg would suggest there was something more in it, some deeper meaning. He told himself the ever-innocent John thought nothing of it at all; he was watching the adventure unfold onscreen.

Alastair watched, too. It was hokum, but it warmed and renewed him. Jo Grant wasn't wearing a short skirt in this, for some stupid reason, but instead had on a tightly fitting tunic that accentuated her pert little tits. Two zips were begging to be undone. She was as incandescently gorgeous as he remembered, as she ventured out of the magical Tardis console room into the weird tropical jungle night of another world. He could just imagine, as he had done as a kid, getting his tongue between her thighs, the sort of sounds she would make. She had a sort of innocence he wanted to ruin – and with that thought, he glanced unconsciously back toward John, who turned to look at him as if sensing him. "Enjoying it?" he said.

Alastair smiled, a little guiltily. "Yeah, thanks," he said. He wondered, could the other man feel he had a stiffy through that single point of contact?

When the episode ended, John got up and went to a wardrobe in the corner. "I want to show you something," he said, and retrieved a set of clothes: an opera cloak, a frock coat, and a frill-fronted shirt. "Recognize it?"

"Pertwee's costume. At last," said Alastair, in some amazement.

"Try it on," said John. "You said you needed a change."

Alastair's lips were dry. "It won't fit me," he said.

"Neither does your uniform any more, big guy. Come on."

Alastair was trapped. He was also supremely touched, which made it worse. He got to his feet. No going back now. Slowly he undid the webbing and belts around his waist and shoulders. He put them carefully on the hotel desk. His big army boots were already by the side of the bed, of course, but now he took off the army gaiters that had been so hard to track down when he was putting the costume together. The vintage, camouflage combat smock fastened with four poppers. Top, two, three, four.

Having watched this far in silence, John turned away now, as if preserving Al's modesty. Al draped the smock carefully over the hotel desk, took a deep breath, then walked over to John and slid the braces off his shoulders. He felt it was like undoing a woman's suspenders. John's grey herringbone trousers now sat loose on the curve of his bum, black underwear on show, almost as exciting as skin.

It wasn't exactly that Al wanted to see John naked, though, as wanted to undress him. To touch him, please him, see what he did. So long, he thought, as he hadn't misread everything, each impulse darting between one man and the other.

He stepped closer to John's rear, reached around to his shirt-front and ran a hand lightly over his stomach, down further, further. "Ah," he said, with satisfaction, feeling what bulged so hot and hard in the fabric under his touch.

No, it seemed he'd read the signs aright.

He'd never touched a cock that wasn't his own, and this one felt bigger than his. He ran thumb and forefinger up and down the shaft and over the big bulb of the head, in curiosity. It was just the same way he had looked at John downstairs in the bar, searching his profile, trying to know him through his body. He was fascinated by this man, enlivened and excited in his curiosity, as he hadn't been by anyone else for years: the sweetness, the nerdishness, and the way he looked at Alastair.

The way he shuddered and sighed at Alastair's touch.

"Turn around," he instructed, stepping smartly away, military style.

"Yes, sir," John replied, mischievously, but obeying. In the light of the TV screen, his eyes glinted, but the red silk bowtie beneath that oh-so clean-shave chin made him look as buttoned-down as a librarian from another era. Alastair moved closer to undo the necktie, and one erection touched another through two sets of trousers. He sprang back as if a spark of electricity had jumped between them.

"Take off the tie," he said.

John, swallowing, assented with a polite move of the head, and carefully unwound the knots, unravelling it in a single strand of red from around his throat. Awkward, suddenly, he looked for where to put it – then dumped it on the floor.

Alastair was already aching to feel their two hard cocks touching again. Slowly he closed in upon the younger man, reaching for the top button of his shirt, and bam, he felt it happen: contact. There was something addictive about the feel of muscle on muscle, odd shapes sliding one against another, the trouser material between, neither knowing which way the other would move when he pressed, when he thrust, when he ground down hard with his hips. Little expressions of pleasure appeared in John's face, as Alastair slowly undid his shirt, and John reached across now and undid the rough army uniform that had been confining Alastair's body all day. Now their arms were almost fighting one another, impeding the other's movements, as they raced to undress one another. Alastair had the advantage, and as soon as he had the shirt off, he laid it carefully on the bed as if it were a religious vestment.

Then he sat on the edge of the bed and studied John's naked torso: slender, hairless, goose-pimply, his pink nipples standing stiff and hard. Alastair couldn't resist rubbing his cock at the sight. John, by turn, was watching him do this with evident pleasure. The still surface of a lake had finally been broken.

"Gorgeous," grunted Alastair, the experience still new to him.

"Really? No." John looked away suddenly, then back at him. "I can't believe – I mean, I knew I wanted you as soon as I saw you. But when you said you had a son …"

Alastair put his hands on his head as if surrendering. "I've never done this before, don't know what it is. It's you, John." I want to ruffle you, he thought. I want to shake you. I want to put my tongue between your legs and see what noises you make.

On an impulse, he slid to his knees and tugged the trousers carefully down to reveal the bulge in his underwear. It was an even bigger bulge than he'd suspected – it went right through the Y-fronts and stuck out the other side, the sledgehammer cockhead pressed stickily against John's thigh. It seemed to burn with the heat of a lighter flame, and the smell was bittersweet as lilies. He stuck out his tongue, unsure what was best to do with it, then got stuck in, running it right the way around, so that for a moment it lifted the cockhead from John's thigh, and for a moment, he saw what a task it would be to take it in his mouth.

The noises John made, even at this little pressure, were gratifyingly impolite.

Alastair put his fingers inside the Y-fronts waistband and slid them steadily down, the fabric sliding over John's shaft, then bumping over the head of his cock. Alastair looked up to see John's expression, not thinking what happens when a hard cock is suddenly unleashed: it flipped up and smacked him in the face, making them both laugh. Alastair quickly wrapped his mouth around it and began to blow him, enthusiastically but not exactly expertly.

Slow down, he told himself. Remember how you like it. Remember the best blowjob you ever got, and do it again.

If he'd imagined this situation before it happened, he'd have expected John's extra inches to make him feel inferior. Instead, it excited him more. John looked such a nice boy. It was, he'd heard, the quiet ones you wanted to watch. It was somehow satisfying for this long, fat prick to be sitting in the trousers of an unostentatious cult TV fan, like a great priapic secret, than the big "I Am's" at Alastair's gym.

He didn't consciously think of any of this. He was too busy working out how a man accommodated a thing this size in his throat, and where John liked best to licked and clasped, and how to tease. Thoughts of teasing made him reach up and rub John's left nipple between finger and thumb, the way he'd roll tobacco in a Rizla paper.

'Stop!" John gasped, pushing Alastair away. "You're going too fast," he added, reassuringly. "I don't want to spend before you've even got your, uh, self out."

Alastair sat back on the corner of the bed and unzipped his fly. He pulled out his cock and tugged on it, still half-dressed in his army uniform. John knelt by the bed and ran a wet, muscular tongue up one side of the shaft, swirled round the head, even in the piss slit (I didn't think of doing that, thought Alastair, with a groan of pleasure) and down the other side, right down into the trousers where the root of Al's cock throbbed in a little well of sweat and dark hair. It was good to see him doing that.

Then John's hands were at work elsewhere: unbuttoning the trousers, pulling them down around his ankles, feeling the hard muscles at the backs of Alastair's thighs, then undoing the last buttons of the army shirt, running a hand across Alastair's broad, deep chest, working the other hand on his cock.

"I don't want to speak out of turn," he said, perspiration dampening his long, floppy fringe, "but how do you feel about making my convention weekend and getting fucked?"

In years to come, when Alastair revisited this night, either for romantic reasons or with his dick in his hand, he often wondered where he found the courage to say yes. At last he decided it was in a spirit of pure excitement, a big 'yes' to new experiences – and the strength to say 'yes' came from the trust he had in John. That and a desire to see how far John would go.

Off John went, a rubber stretched tight over his wide, hot pink fuck-stick, a fistful of lube making it gleam in the TV screen light. Off he went, his tongue tickling and tasting Alastair's arse, preparing him thoughtfully, but with a serious, impatient look on his face. Off he went: on the brink, over the brink, steadily deeper, down to the balls. Off he went, thrusting slowly, licking and kissing Al's chest: each individual chest hair seemed to have a kiss, and both hands, still dappled with lube, were on Al's dick.

And Al's heart was thudding under his breastbone, just where John's mouth was. And did it begin to thud in sympathy with John's slender hips, his thick cock, thudding into Alastair? When he tried to remember afterwards, all he could remember was the 'yes,' the excitement, the serious look on John's face – becoming more serious, almost angry, as the strokes beat faster, wilder. The hard, solid muscle Al had begun to sculpt of himself, the blocks and globes of granite, rippled and shook as he was fucked, as the young man fucked him, as the slightly-built young man hooked his arms around John's legs and fucked, fucked, fucked him.

And then in one controlled move he pulled his dick out of Alastair and rolled off the condom; he was up on top of Alastair, he was holding their dicks together, his hand moving with a dexterity Alastair couldn't picture, it was a blur of pleasure.

They kissed, they were grunting, yodeling in each other's hot, flushed faces.

And in the silence afterward they were smiling again, laughing, and stuck together with cum.

81

This wasn't even the moment of true courage. That came afterwards, when they were cleaned up and sitting by one another in the dark, just as they had been, thigh touching thigh, but now hand in hand as well. They were both staring at their entwined fingers, and John said: "Well, this has been a new adventure."

Alastair sighed. "It's been a missing adventure, for too long. Thank you."

After a pause, John said: "It doesn't have to end in Bournemouth, you know."

Not wanting to disagree, Alastair said: "What did you have in mind?"

"We could run away together. Tonight. Now."

Alastair laughed. "Wheesht! You've been watching too much *Doctor Who!*"

John gave him a funny look, let go his hand and climbed off the bed. Alastair's heart began to race. Fuck, no, you got it wrong! This is supposed to be a sweet goodbye – but what do you say to an invitation like that? His mind began to race, trying to think of ways to apologize, to calm the troubled water.

And John opened the wardrobe door again, and an otherworldly light spilled out. Alastair could hear a weird pulsing within: the sound of adventure brewing.

"Next stop, the planet Spiridon," whispered John, his face ghostly with shadows. "What do you say?"

What could Alastair say? "What about my son?"

"Not my type. Too young. Besides," John replied, putting a finger to his lips, "He has adventures of his own now."

The wire was tightening in Alastair again, his pulse was quickening, his cock was stiff as a poker again, and the hairs on the back of his neck were up. He examined his options, stood up and gave a smart salute. "Yes, sir," he said.

Alastair MacRae could never resist a good cliffhanger. Who can?

BRAINIAC NYMPHOMANIAC
By Rob Rosen

Rob Rosen (www.therobrosen.com), hails from San Francisco. He's a nine-time novelist, four-time anthologist, and 300+ published short story writer.

It was one of those forgotten wings of the science building, dark and musty, cobwebbed and dust-laden. When the new center was built, they'd run out of money to tear the old one down, so they relegated the ancient professors with tenure there, they and the scientists with fringe experiments who barely stayed afloat with meager funding, stocking it with equipment that no one else wanted.

That's where I found him, huddled in a corner, his back to me, face pressed up tight to a microscope that was state of the art back in the eighties. His lab coat, I noticed, had turned from white to gray, his hair an unkempt mess of brown curls, large black glasses visible on either side of his downturned, hidden face.

I tapped him on the shoulder. He seemed not to notice. I tapped him again. "Uh, excuse me."

He lifted an index finger up in the air, paused, turned a knob on the microscope, and replied, "Just a sec."

The sec went by, a minute more, then another. "Um, hello?" I tried again.

He sighed and lifted his head. Given the surroundings, the history of this place he was relegated to, I expected him to be an old man. But when he turned and adjusted his glasses, that's not at all what I found.

"Yes?" he said. "What is it?"

"Oh," I managed in reply.

"Oh?" he echoed.

I nodded. "I, uh, thought you'd be older."

He shrugged. "Older than what?"

"Than you are."

In fact, he was probably in his mid-twenties, noticeably short, impossibly thin, enveloped by his lab coat, swallowed whole by it, in fact. He was scruffy, his face all angles, an Adam's apple that was more lemon-sized, large ears to hold up his equally large glasses, and eyes so blue they sparkled like sapphires in the fluorescent light that illuminated the corner of the small lab we found ourselves in.

"You lost me," he said. "Do I know you?" He shook his head. "Well, no, wait, I couldn't know you, right? If I did then I'd be the age that I am and not older. Unless we know each other from the net, the Wiki, some sort of social media. Then we could know each other and you might still assume I'm older than I am, which I'm not, clearly."

He started to continue with his ramblings before I stopped him with my hand, which I held out in greeting. "Lou Ferrigno," I informed. "Pleasure to meet you, Professor Hastings."

He chuckled. "Lou Ferrigno? I'd imagine you older as well. Taller. Certainly bulkier. A tad more deaf. Better not make you angry, right?" His face went fierce, or at least as fierce as possible, as he scrunched it up and flexed his birdlike chest, again as much as possible. "Hulk smash!"

I forced a smile. It was an old joke, my name being the same as that kitschy actor's. I was accustomed to it by then. Still, when he grabbed my hand in his, a weak shake administered, as flesh met flesh, a spark of gamma radiation did unexpectedly run through me.

"Wrong Lou Ferrigno," I told him.

"No, right Lou Ferrigno," he said. "You being Lou Ferrigno and all, I mean. It would be wrong if your name was, say, Bruce Banner." He smiled at his ingenuity. I smiled in return because the grin made him somehow cute in a nerdy sort of way. "In any case, I don't know you, Lou Ferrigno, or the actor that bears your name, though I did meet Stan Lee at a Comic-Con once, back in 2008, after waiting in line for three hours and twenty-seven minutes."

Again I stopped him. "I'm here to write an article about you, Professor Hastings. Didn't the department let you know?"

He squinted his eyes and seemed to look beyond me. When he again focused, he replied, "They don't inform me of much, Mister Ferrigno. I think they prefer it if we kept a respectable distance from one another. A weekly email perhaps. A paycheck every other week. Christmas party every year."

"Must be a big shindig, what with the department being so large and all."

His shrug amped up a notch. "Don't know. Never been."

I wasn't surprised. "Anyway, I'm doing an article on the University's commitment to cancer research, and your name came up." I noticed that his hand was still in mine. Did he simply miss human contact or did he forget that it was there? Hard to tell. "That is your specialty, is it not?"

He nodded. The grin returned. Strangely, my cock pulsed at the sight of it. It did seem to stand out, after all. "That it is," he replied. "Canine cancer research."

I scratched my head. "Related to throat cancer, gum cancer? Something like that?"

"Wrong canine," he said. "Related to dog cancer." He straightened his glasses. "Canines, a family of mammals, including dogs, jackals, wolves and foxes, typically having a bushy tail, a long muzzle, and erect ears." His face suddenly seemed to go red, a molten flush working its way up his thin neck. "Sorry."

Again I scratched my head before tilting it sideways. "For?"

The red turned crimson. "You know, for saying, um, erect." The word came out in a hushed whisper.

I mirrored his previous shrug. "I'm more a bushy tail man, myself."

He laughed, the sound boyish, high-pitched, but delightful just the same. "Funny," he hiccupped, then caught himself. "Wait, really?" He shook his head and adjusted his billowing lab coat. "Never mind. Not my business. In any case, yes, Mister Ferrigno, cancer research. For dogs. The funding is obviously there, meager though it is, but the university generally prefers to keep the interest up for the human variety. Hence my lab's location. Hence, I assume, the reason they seem to have neglected to inform me about you."

I nodded. Made sense. "Or why I didn't know of your specialty in advance." I stared at him. He stared at me. He looked nervous. I felt nervous. And then I went two steps in reverse, figuratively speaking. "Um, 'really' and 'never mind' what?"

"Excuse me?" he asked as he cleared his throat and cast his eyes downward.

"You said, 'wait, really,' and 'never mind'. In reference to what, Professor?"

His massive Adam's apple bobbed. Again he looked up at me, spectacular eyes boring through. "Bushy tail."

"Huh?"

He moved in closer. I could suddenly smell his aftershave, detect the person beneath the lab coat. "You said you liked bushy tails. Canine bushy tails?"

"Ah," I ahed. "No. Human."

"Really?"

I laughed. "You said that already." I also moved in closer. "Why, do you?"

"Do I what?"

"Prefer bushy tails? Human bushy tails." And to further elucidate, I added, "Male bushy tails."

His grin went lopsided. "On, um, on occasion," he squeaked out.

"On occasion?" I echoed. "How occasionally?"

The last gulp was the deepest by far. "When, you know, the occasion presents itself."

"Which is when?"

He sighed. "Rarely."

"Shame," I cooed. "I bet you have a rather nice bushy tail."

"Really?"

"You should try to stop saying that."

"Sorry," he apologized. "Nervous response. I mean, look at you and look at me." He had a point. We were very Clark Kent versus Superman, suffice it to say.

I tickled the underside of his chin. "I am looking. I like what I see. And is your tail, as we've been saying, bushy?" I closed the remainder of the gap that separated us. My mouth brushed his, that spark of ours returning, enough to start a brush fire with. "Show me," I rasped.

"Real ..." he stared to say, and then corrected it with, "You want to see my ass, Mister Ferrigno? Here? Now?"

I smiled and kissed him again. His impossibly soft lips trembled beneath my own, but the kiss was returned in kind just the same. "Well, I'm here and you're here, and there doesn't seem to be anyone else here, so now would be the ideal time, don't you think?"

He grinned. "Well, your hypothesis does sound reasonable enough."

"Really?"

His grin turned to laughter as he walked to the door and locked it. "Just in case." He looked even more nervous when he headed back my way, though resolute just the same. The blush returned as he peeled off his lab coat, revealing the slim man beneath. He was dressed in gray slacks, high-waters, and an odd looking button-down in muted pastels. "I've, uh, never done this before."

I took a front row seat, a lab stool, and replied, "What, gotten undressed at work in front of a complete stranger who's about to do a piece on you for a large multi-city newspaper?"

He touched fingertip to nose. "All of that," he said. "Any of that."

"And why now?" I asked, watching intently as he shucked off his sneakers and rolled off his black socks.

"Well," he said, moving in closer, his hands pausing at the top button of his shirt, "you're the only man ever to ask me."

"Pity," I said, pushing down on the boner in my jeans. "And please proceed. Bushy tail time."

"Right." I saw that his hands were shaking as he unfastened one button after the next, a dense patch of chest hair revealed, curly, brown. The material parted, two tiny pink nipples jutting forth, swirled in fuzz.

"Pull 'em," I said.

He stopped unbuttoning and nodded. He gripped the nubs in his hands and gave them a tug, a twist, an eager torque. He moaned at his ministrations, and I moaned in harmony with him, staring hungrily at the lump that had since formed in his slacks. Another button popped open, another after that, tummy revealed, not an ounce of fat, all dense muscle and even denser hair. Perhaps he was part canine himself, I imagined. A wolf or a jackal, whatever that was. He certainly had the ears for it.

The shirttails came out of his slacks, the shirt opened and removed, set down on the lab bench. His shoulders were hairy, arms as well, pits to match, all sexy as hell. His fingers again paused when they reached for the zipper to his slacks.

"What is it?" I asked.

"It's just …"

I smiled. "Nervous?"

He nodded. "Not exactly, uh, professorial."

"Says who?" I countered with. "Maybe everyone's doing it. Maybe you're just late to the game. If you showed up for a Christmas party every now and again, perhaps you'd know."

He didn't respond. Instead, the zipper came down, the sound like a swarm of bees that made my head swim and my prick leak. My throat went Saharan when he popped open the button and the slacks fell to the floor before they were promptly kicked off.

His legs were thin like the rest of him, rife with hair, his boxers white and three-ring tenting something fierce.

"Almost there," I cooed.

Again he nodded, gulped, wiped the sweat off his forehead. "Um, right." And down came the boxers and out popped a fifth limb of a prick, swaying before coming to a standstill, curved just a tad to the left and slightly up. The head was fat as a plumb and heavily leaking, the shaft long, thin and veiny, the balls gargantuan, hairy, hanging so low they were practically in their own zip code.

I lifted my hand in the air and swirled my index finger, indicating that he should turn around. He did, grabbing onto the work bench as he jutted his ass out, legs wide.

Bushy, as it turned out, was a gross understatement.

He had a beautiful ass, petite, well-sculpted, two small orbs of tight flesh covered in down, the crack especially, his lower back even more so. His legs were bouncing as he stood there. I think I was pushing him well beyond his usual boundaries, but it seemed he was eager to be pushed.

"Spread 'em," I requested.

He nodded and grabbed his cheeks, the flesh parted, hole revealed, hair-rimmed, crinkled, pink. I hopped off my stool and quick-stepped it his way. I crouched down and placed my face up to his chute. I took a deep whiff of him. He smelled of musk and sweat, of cock and ass. In his lab coat, he was a nerdy professor; out of it, out of all his clothes, he was a hot, little, hairy man.

I licked his hole with gusto. He trembled and arched his back, shoving his tiny ass into my face. "Mmm," he hummed.

"Ditto," I agreed, licking and lapping and nibbling at his tender chute. I reached between his thin thighs and grabbed his dick. It throbbed in my grip, pulsed. I aimed it down as far as it would go. He widened his stance and grunted, while I in turn pushed my head up and through, sucking on the bulbous head, precum slamming into the back of my throat like a bullet.

He pumped his dick into my mouth. I stared up at the sinewy length of him, through the jungle of hair. His was staring down, watching me watch him, playing with his eraser-tipped nipples as he did so.

"You're very good at that, Mister Ferrigno," he commented.

I popped his prick out of my mouth. It hovered there, slick with spit, an entity unto itself. "Thank you, Professor," I replied. "Would you like to return the favor?"

He nodded, eagerly. "Please."

I stood from my crouched position. He turned around and stared up at me, orbs of blue framed in thick glass. I got undressed while he watched, then held him in my arms as we swapped some heavy spit, our cocks dueling down below.

He moved away, and I did the same. I got on the floor, prone, face up, cock up. He walked around me, his small feet on either side of my face. From this position, he looked taller, thinner, hairier, if at all possible, his dick like a tree branch, jutting far, far out. And then he fell forward onto all fours, his ass in my face, his mouth above my steely prick.

Down he went, gobbling it in one fell swoop. What he lacked in style he made up for in enthusiasm, in fervor. I in turn ran my hands through his soft, brown down, massaging his thin thighs before parting his cheeks again. The holy trinity lay spread out before me: hairy hole and dangling balls and hovering cock.

I pulled his ass into my face and reamed him out, my deft tongue running laps around his track before ramming in completely. His body trembled as I parted him. Mine did the same as he took my cock to his throat's hilt.

I moved my head away and gazed at my work. Spit dripped from his hole. I lapped it up with my index finger and then slid it inside of him. He moaned, loudly, and arched his back. My free hand rose up, around his narrow waist, and took hold of his prick. He sucked while I stroked and fingered, both of us sweating now, my backside suctioned to the floor.

Out came my finger, in went two. He was now tugging my balls as his mouth went up and down, up and down. A Hoover couldn't have sucked any better, and my cock felt like it was on fire, ready to erupt at any moment. Still, I held back, keeping my release at bay as best I could while I stroked the cum up from his mammoth, swaying balls.

Out came my prick from his mouth in an audible pop. "Three's the charm," he panted, rocking his ass into my probing fingers.

"You sure?" I asked. I mean, he felt super tight already. Plus, my fingers were on the large side, and, well, nothing about him, besides his cock, could say the same.

"Three," he rasped. "Three. Fuck me with three."

I grinned. "If you say so, Professor."

His mouth went to work again on my dick, aided by his capable hand. A million volts of adrenaline shot through me as he jacked and sucked, sucked and jacked. Doing as he asked, I removed my digging duo, hocked a lugie into them, and made it a tunneling trio. In they slid, the pressure from his hole palpable. Still, he took it, growling and groaning all the while, his cock impossibly thick in my stroking mitt.

He was close. I was closer.

One final thrust of my hand into him, one last jack of his cock, two more sucks of his mouth, and that was all she wrote. I spewed down his throat. He rained cum onto my chest and belly, a torrent of it that splattered hotly before dripping over my sides. Both of us moaned up a storm as we shot and shot, our cocks in spewing sync, bodies quaking until my vision blurred.

I removed my fingers and spanked his hairy ass. The sound echoed throughout the lab. He removed his mouth and swallowed my load, licking his lips as he sought out any errant pearly drops.

I chuckled. "Bushy ass. Check," I said, spanking him again. "Ready for that interview now?"

He coughed and then laughed as he pushed himself off of me and onto the floor, his pigeon chest and tight belly rapidly rising and falling as he stared at the ceiling. "Now?" he exhaled.

I nodded and rolled onto my side as I ran my hand through his dense matting of chest hair. "Well, that is why I came here, no pun intended."

He grinned. "Um, sounded sort of intended to me."

I returned his grin with one of my own. "Okay, somewhat intended then."

And so I asked the questions, and he answered them, proudly. I taped him with a recorder I brought, which left my free hands able to explore his hirsute expanse of flesh and muscle, soon bringing his cock back to life. When the tape was full, he shot again, eyelids fluttering, the sea of blue temporarily disappearing as a flood of aromatic spunk gushed out.

"Man," I said, duly impressed.

He nodded. "Been a while, I suppose."

But I put an end to that.

The interview, in fact, went on for several more sessions, over many more days, tape after tape filling up, him and his hole insatiable during that time. I fucked him with abandon as I asked about his work, what he hoped to achieve, what he had achieved thus far, which was substantial. He answered all my questions and took every thrust and stroke and suck with an ability that left me weak.

When it was all over and the interview and the article were released, I continued fucking him, happily, giddily, relentlessly. Continued even when the money started pouring in, donors lining up to fund his work. Even when his lab got moved, from the old annex to the new one, when his equipment was replaced, all of it the best money could buy.

"Thank you, Mister Ferrigno," he gasped, months later, my cock buried deep, deep inside his stupendously little ass.

"Hulk smash!" I replied, plowing into his hairy hole. "Hulk smash good!"

"He sure does," came the panted reply. "Really."

A THREE-GEEK GIG
By R. W. Clinger

R. W. Clinger can be reached at www.rwclinger.com
and by e-mail at rwclinger@verizon.net, and Twitter
and Facebook.

Geek Log: April 3, 20 –

Milford Majeski's making one of his biological documentaries again. This one is on butterflies and how they gestate. He says the weirdest things that all start with the letter C: chrysalis, conical, and cremaster. I don't understand what the hell he's talking about and have to look the words up in a dictionary on my phone. He's on a C-kick today because he mentions the Columbian Skipper, the Callippe Fritillary, the Common Checkered Skipper, the California Hairstrike, and the Common Sooty-Wing, which are all types of butterflies. His short video lasts about seven minutes long, and he fidgets with his cellphone thereafter, pressing buttons and uploading the short to the other thousand subscribers on a website called Ponder This, Ponder That.

Today he's dressed as Spiderman, minus the mask. Yesterday it was the Hulk, but I didn't do an entry in my Geek Log yesterday. Whatever. And who knows which superhero he will be tomorrow. I'm thinking Superman, maybe. Milford's thin enough to pull off the Spider-man look. The blue, red, and black costume clings to his somewhat medium-muscled body with its perfect dents and curves. I can study his biceps, abs, and muscular thighs without error. Although he's five-ten, the superhero costume makes him look like he's six-two or -three. Milford's not bad to look at; the reason I maybe study him. He has onyx-colored hair, Mediterranean blue eyes, and a set of Colgate white choppers that have worn braces when he was in his early teens. He weighs approximately one-fifty, is almost gangly, but in a sexy way, and wears a pair of gold-framed glasses that went out of style in 1990, the year he was born.

What I find most intriguing about my roommate is the package between his legs. His Spidey unitard clings to his center like plastic wrap and leaves nothing to one's queer imagination regarding such an area. Milford's dick must be six inches soft and almost two inches wide. I'm talking a baguette is crammed between his thighs, arching a little to the left, pointing diagonally downward. And his balls aren't much smaller, two croquette-size orbs accessorizing his meaty cock. He's a tasty treat to look at and sort of hot in a deranged notion. Would I do him? In a second. Does he know this? The intelligent bastard doesn't have a clue.

Required note: I like the black-haired geek a little too much. Shame on me. It's never polite to cross a line of friendship, though, is it? Then again, going against nature is something practiced every day by humans. Hmmmm...

Log End.

# # # # #

Kirk Kirkland – yes, his parents really named him this – lives in the apartment with Milford and me on Chelsea Street. He's the nerdy comedian, mathematician, and Mensa member with too much testosterone. Frankly, he's always horsing around and acts like he's twelve instead of twenty-four. The guy's a sexy gingerhead with alluring blue eyes, freckles, and a compact ass that I would like to smack (or tap) once or twice, whatever he would prefer. Kirk's a total geek, but not like Milford. He's funny, and fun to be around. Kirk operates a secret club of redheaded ninjas. Hot gingers pay yearly dues to play with long sticks, drink Mountain Dew, and think they're a rare Japanese cult. Whatever his gig is, Kirk is not boring by any means. And to prove such a statement, I am not at all surprised when he finds me alone in my bedroom, closes the door behind him, and whispers, "Hey, Robby, I need to talk to you."

"About what?" I'm sprawled over my bed in a pair of running shorts, knee-high socks, and a T-shirt that says NERD across my flat pecs. I'm reading through a stack of English essays written by advanced ninth graders. The topic is none other than *A Catcher in the Rye*. How cliché is this? Too cliché to even talk about.

Kirk takes in my blond looks. Blond mussed hair. Blond eyebrows. Pale skin. I'm a geek all the way, just like my roommates. "About Milford."

I remove my glasses, place them on the stack of essays in front of me, rub my eyes, and say, "What about him?"

He leans into me and continues to whisper, "His birthday is next week. I'm thinking we do the bed gag on him again. What do you say?"

The bed gag entails taping Milford to his bed, strapping duct tape over his mouth, ankles, wrists, and leaving him inside his room for most of his birthday, which will inevitably be ruined. It's a little brutal, a little hysterical, but loads of fun. Exactly what two friends are expected to do, of course.

Long story short, Kirk and I have lived with Milford for the last four years. We don't bully Milford, but we do pick on him, whenever we can. He's like a toy for us, if you want to know the truth. We have fun with him like a Ken doll or a gaming system. In the past, while he was sleeping, we dressed him up as Princess Leah from *Star Wars* and carried his body – because he's like the dead when he sleeps – to the front of the apartment building and put him on the sidewalk, leaving him there in nothing more than a pair of mint green boxers.

"He'll kill us if we do that again," I say, being serious for once.

"I have something else up my sleeve this year."

"What's that?" I ask, intrigued with his coyness.

He's dressed in a pair of shorts and a T-shirt, just like me, grabs his cock through the cotton, and says, "Someone needs to get laid. That's what's up. I plan to show that guy a good time with your help. Once you go red, you …"

"You become misled," I finish his statement, rolling my eyes. I shake my head and say, "This is not a good plan, Kirk. What are we going to do, rape him? I won't let that happen."

He admits with an ear to ear grin, "I was thinking of getting your help to jack that big dick of his off."

I grin, half-tempted to join him. My sane side kicks in and I say, "That sounds illegal."

He rubs his cock, which isn't as big as Milford's, since I sucked it once when I was twenty and totally shit-faced on cheap beer, but it was plump enough to get a healthy fuck accomplished. "We'll get his consent first. How does that sound? If he doesn't want a treat from us, we won't take advantage of him. I promise."

"He'll be taped to his bed. Will he have a choice?"

"We'll give him a choice. He can get a handjob for his birthday or his ass fucked by either you or me. Hell, he can even have both options if he wants. It doesn't really matter as long as he gets off and blows a birthday load."

I shake my head and laugh. "You are not right, Kirk."

"Never was. Never will be."

He's semi-hard between his legs. The outline in his running shorts is impressive, but not like Milford's. I think about his proposed gig, realize that it's pretty harmless with Milford's consent, and tell Kirk, "Count me in. This could be fun."

Not even ten minutes later I hear him on a solid jerk-fest inside his bedroom. He's watching some porn on his computer, jacking off to a string of Steven Daigle scenes. Kirk huffs and puffs for twenty minutes and eventually shoots his wad over his flat and freckled chest, becoming spent. Afterwards, he takes a shower, shovels leftover Chinese into his mouth, and goes to his red-headed ninja club thing on the other side of Hillsdale, living a content life.

Geek Log: April 5, 20 –
The biologist is at work again. I really don't know what the fuck the guy is doing. Something with two frogs and flies this time. Who knows? I comprehend adverbs, run-on sentences, and hanging participles, but I can't get the gist of his short video with the frogs. This time he talks about vegetal cytoplasm, a diploid zygotic nucleus, and blastopores. It screams NERD all over it. It screams SOCIAL MISFIT. It screams I NEED TO GET FUCKED BY ONE OF MY GEEKY ROOMMATES.

He's dressed as the Hulk and talks about an algebraic formula for what seems like seven years. I can feel my hair grow grey and arthritis form in my fingers; this is how long his rambling occurs. So I decide to have a little one-on-one chat with him in his bedroom, just to make him understand that he's about as boring as watching tar dry in the sun. It's my turn to ramble, and I'm pretty skilled at it:

106

"Milford, you need to know something. Listen to me. If you're going to do these videos about biology, you're going to have to give them some life. Personality is needed. They need some spice, man. I can't handle them anymore. I know you've been doing the videos for three years now, but they are starting to sound monotonous. They reek of lifeless whatever. I suggest you step it up a notch. Get a talking dog to help you out. Get a stud named Mr. Muscles to be your sidekick. Trust me, you've got to do something more exciting."

"Stop," he says, which sort of surprises me because he's never told me to stop anything for as long as I've known him.

So I stop rambling. "What?"

He takes his glasses off, and I see someone handsome, charming, and rather cute. He looks like a Prince in a Walt Disney animated movie. "Forget about my videos. Concentrate on something else."

What he does next just about knocks me to his bedroom floor with shock, not horror. He pulls his Twinkie T-shirt off and drops it to the floor. His jeans are unbuttoned and pushed down to his ankles. He steps out of the denim and removes his baggy boxers that look like something out of 1954, and stands buck ass naked in front of me. "What do you think of this?"

He's beautiful in an odd way. Sort of like how an ugly duckling might be beautiful. His chest is dotted with a few sexy moles and his navel is dented ever so slightly. There are small abs that make up his belly and his nipples are a bright pink. He has a black trail of treasure hair under his navel and it falls into a V-patch of trimmed pubic hair above his deflated dick. The guy's cock is six inches limp between his legs, cut with a mushroom cap. His thighs are hairless as well as his dangling balls. He's not porn star material, but he's definitely boyfriend material and sexy. Adorable comes to mind rather than steamy hot. Frankly, he's a modest and good looking guy in an odd way, and I'm fixated by him.

"What's that Bruno Mars song?" I ask him.

"Grenade."

"No."

"Locked out of Heaven."

"No."

"Uptown Funk."

"No."

"Just the Way You Are."

"Bingo!" I say, snap, and point an index finger at him. "That's it. And that's how I like you. Just the way you are, Milford."

"Come here," he says, steps up to me, wraps me in his arms, presses his naked body against my clothed one, and plants a kiss on my lips.

For an unexpected kiss, it's earth-shaking. There's nothing wimpy about it, if the truth be shared. His execution is not slippery, haphazard, or overpowering. I don't know where he has learned to kiss – maybe band camp when he was in high school – but he knows exactly what he's doing and rocks my world.

It's kind of disappointing that the kiss ends, and he steps away from me. I'm a touch windblown and breathless, enjoying the moment with him. Such reactions do not prevent me from asking, "So now what happens between us, Milford?"

And he shocks me with, "Get on your knees, make me hard, and blow me."

So I learn that Milford has some animal in him, and he likes to be in sexual control. I'm on my knees, stroke his thumping and massive cock with my left hand, bring it to life, make it hard, and decide to suck the tip of it like a baby's bottle.

He moans in front of me, brushes both palms through my head of hair, begins to pant, murmurs something about wanting to ram his dick between my lungs, and ...

"Milford! ... Milford Majeski!" his mother yells, banging her plump fist on the apartment's front door. "Milford, I can hear you in there!"

With a force that can only be derived by Greek Gods, he pushes me away, off his boner, which snaps against his navel and abs because it is hard as steel. He turns red from head to toe, embarrassed by his mother's surprise visit, and rushes to the bathroom with his clothes. On his trek, showing off his tight and fuckable ass, he calls over his right shoulder, "Be a friend and deal with her, Robby."

And so it is done. I deal with Emma Majeski, a social worker at the nearby mental facility, like the good friend I am, prepare an afternoon drink – she likes her martinis and never turns one down, I have learned through the years – for her while her bio-geek son dresses in the bathroom, deflating his erection some way or another.

Required note: I don't share this afternoon scene of bedlam and cock-sucking with Kirk. Some things I like to keep to myself, of course. Who doesn't do this? No one I know of.

Log End.

# # # # #

Milford's birthday comes, and if Kirk's plan is executed with proficiency, which it surely will be, Milford will also come. The three of us do what any nerd wants to do on his birthday: visit the local computer store, game at Gamelandia, spend an hour in Pender's Comic Book Store, and go to the movies to see the newest *Star Trek* installment. We have dinner at Milford's favorite Thai place after the movie, return to the apartment close to midnight, and kick Kirk's sex-plan in motion for all three of us to enjoy.

There are no drugs shared when the three of us get back to the apartment on Chelsea Street. Chemicals are not mixed to create a cloud of meth-like substance to get high on. We do not consume one beer after the next and become sloppy and blitzed. Truth is, Kirk forgets his sex-plan of blowing Milford for his birthday gift and heads to bed, claiming he's exhausted. I also head to bed. Milford ends up in his room and watches queer porn on his laptop, becoming hard, bent on blowing his load and ...

I don't know what time of the morning it is, but there's light brimming the day and the birthday boy pokes me with a finger in my side (or maybe it's his dick, I really don't know), and he nudges me, whispering, "Robby, are you awake?"

I'm not awake. Fact is, I'm dreaming of fucking the surfer brothers, Evan and Eric Geiselman, getting my geek on with them and acting like a porn star. I stir awake on my queen-size mattress, feel a boner between my legs, and Milford's boner against my lips, attempting to press its rounded cap into the fold of my mouth.

Positioned above me, Milford says, "Robby, you need to suck me off. I can't handle the pent load I've got going on between my legs."

So I do what a good friend does: I open my mouth, allow him to slide his Titanic-size cock down my throat, and let him use some hyper hip-thrusts against my face, slapping his balls off my chin. I admit, it's not a bad way to wake up. Being gagged isn't fun, but it is when your geeky, big-dicked roommate accomplishes such a naughty act in the morning's light.

111

What unfolds in my room is porn-perfect. He rocks his hips to and fro, holds the back of my skull with an extended palm, grunts, murmurs, and growls a few times. His ball sack slaps against my chin numerous times, and he plows my throat with his erection, having every intention of getting off and unloading his cream this morning.

Heavy panting ensues on his part. And I slurp, gag, and feel my throat go numb because of his diligent labor. We're at it for maybe four minutes straight when Milford quickly pulls his chunk of dick out of my mouth and freezes next to the bed. Saliva pools at the corners of my mouth. And both of us stare at my bedroom's doorway, observing an interrupting intruder.

Of course, it's the ginger on the opposite side of the room. Kirk Kirkland is naked and handsome with his freckles, pale skin, and fully inflated erection. A wicked grin is spread over his face, which tells me he's horny, and he asks, "What's going on in here?"

It's the birthday boy who says, "We started without you. Hope you don't mind."

"Of course I mind," Kirk says, jacking the upright inches of dick between his legs with his right palm. "Let me in on this geek-action, you two."

His wish becomes a reality this morning. Before I know it, all three of us are in my bed – a blond, a ginger, and a black-haired birthday boy – naked and ready to use each other.

There's nothing geeky about our threesome, I acknowledge. We meld together with some heavy kissing, petting, licks, and hugs. Erections are fondled, chests are gently bitten, and hips are fingered. Lips lock, bottoms are grasped, abs are finger-grazed, and tongues fall into mouths with such ease. There is no organization to what occurs on the bed. Our action is a haphazard and almost clumsy act that causes masculine laughter, a string of groans, and pre-spew to leak out of our dicks, which decorates thighs, stomachs, and nipples.

I don't know what comes over me when I tell the pair to get on their hands and knees and spread their legs open for my tongue-use. Both listen to me, excited because of our sexual threesome, and private birthday party. Milford is on my left with his bony but sexy ass facing me, and Kirk is on my right, showing off a pair of swinging balls between his semi-parted legs. Standing over the two edible looking asses on the bed, I ask, "Are you guys ready for this?"

They reply in unison, eager for my action, "Hell yeah."

I spank them, rub the top of my firm cock against their tight and pink assholes, roll palms and fingers over their droopy balls, and listen to them huff with enjoyment. Following my teasing, I decide to use my tongue on Milford's bottom first because it's his birthday. I rim his pale opening with semi-circles, dot the tip of my extension against his center, and hear him whimper in front of me. Ginger is next. His asshole is decorated with a few spirals of red hair, which is a total turn-on for me and causes the

113

boner between my legs to bob up and down with a mind of its own. I roll my tongue against his puckered hole, lather it with licks, and hear the guy hum unintelligible whatnots in front of me.

After my lick-gig on their bulbous bottoms, Milford demands, "I want both of your cocks inside me at the same time." He climbs off the bed, fetches lube and latex from his bedroom, and returns in a few seconds, handing out more demands. "You two lay on your backs in opposite directions with your legs scissored together. Get your balls to kiss and your cocks upright, stem parallel to stem, so I can ride them and get my rocks off."

I give him a look of puzzlement and say, "It sounds like you've done this before."

"Yeah, it does," Ginger backs me up.

Milford laughs, shakes his head, and admits, "No, but I've always wanted to. Now is my chance, and I'm not about to pass it up."

So Kirk's dick and my dick are both covered with latex and lube, and a happy Milford climbs on the bed and positions himself over our bodies, lowering his ass atop our pulsing flags. His back faces Kirk and I get his front, which suits me just fine since he isn't bad to look at. Milford becomes a bossy big-dicked birthday boy and says to Kirk, "Put your dick inside me first, Kirk."

Kirk listens as he holds his spike up for use.

Milford falls down and over the inflated muscle.

"Now you, Robby," Milford instructs, groaning while taking on the two cocks at the same time.

Kirk huffs, "We're going to hurt you, Milford. Are you sure you want to do this?"

"Fuck yeah," Milford responds, plugged with the two cocks, heaving for breath, groaning, and quivering above us, but taking on the task like a man, not the geek that he really is.

What unfolds on the bed is something out of a Cocky Boys skin flick. Milford takes the ride of his life, whimpering with tears in his eyes, rising and falling on the pair of cocks. He looks like he's surfing above us, balancing his weight over our bodies, and having the time of his life. I try to push my cock inside him, but really can't move on the bed, under him. I'm sure Kirk attempts the same action, but fails, just like me. So Milford does all the work atop our inflated dicks, fucking himself with the geek-pricks, riding the queer road of life, and having a blast celebrating his birthday with two sticks inside his bottom.

Milford's self-pounding is quite the site to see, and I wish that we could digitally tape the event, enjoying it for future viewings. He's a monster on the two dicks, pulverizing his own ass, building friction among the three of us. The horny nerd bounces up and down as if he's riding a bull, puffs for oxygen, perspires like a boxer, and has a look of jubilation on his face, which is comprised of an upturned smile and tears at the edges of his eyes. "Let me have it, guys!" he yells, springing on our tools and accomplishing all the labor. "Fuck me with all you've got!"

The other tenants in the apartment complex can hear us, I conceive. As Milford screams his demands, Kirk howls and woofs, into our three-geek gig this morning. And I too am not quiet, of course, since I holler up at the birthday boy, "Ride them, Milford! Fuck yourself with our shafts! Ride them like a fucking cowboy!"

#

Milford comes first. He rides the cock-train with all his might, bouncing up and down, becoming overjoyed and red-cheeked because of his action. His right palm wraps around the long dick between his legs, and he manhandles the erection with speed, jostling its excess skin up and down. The guy closes his eyes, tightens the cords along his neck because he clamps his teeth together, and provides our threesome with some heavy duty whining, which echoes off the bedroom's walls. As this connection of events unravels, Milford tugs on his stick a few more times, squints, and releases four threads of juice from his cock, which ornaments my navel and the smooth area between my pecs.

Following Milford's sex act, he climbs off our rods and instructs, "Blow your loads on me, guys. That's what I really want for my birthday."

Kirk and I are happy to provide him with a spunk-bath. We kneel on the bed and Milford is positioned on his back between our upright frames. I watch Kirk manhandle the post between his thighs, jockeying it with his left palm. And I know that he is watching me perform the same act, which continues for the next few minutes.

As Kirk and I jerk our dicks, Milford is happy playing with our balls: cupping them, squeezing them, rolling fingers over them, and other physical activities with the sets, occupying his time and enlightening us in doing so.

After ten euphoric-packed minutes of tugging on my own stick, I'm ready to unleash a pent cargo. Sweat flies off my chest, and my hands jack the cock between my thighs, persistent with motion. Elation builds within my frame, and I whisper, "Popping, you two. Can't hold it in." Glistening, white coils of jiz fly out of my spike and nail Milford's forehead, an earlobe, his chin, and parts of his torso.

"Shooting," Kirk announces just a few seconds after my explosion. He bolts his hips forward and backward and unloads his dick-juice, which splatters against his target, anywhere on Milford's body. Huffs and a few grunts escape his semi-opened mouth. And before the three of us known it, Kirk becomes empty, no longer holding man-glue in his balls.

We come on Milford, spraying him down with our bursts. Milford's face and bony chest are covered in goop. White strings of the sticky substance hang from his bottom lip, left nipple, and decorate his navel. More cream spots one of his shoulders, the splay of his neck, and there's a droplet on his forehead.

Milford laughs and says, "You guys rained your spunk all over me."

"It's what you asked for," Ginger says, finishing his stroke-fest with three more tugs.

"I did ask for your loads," Milford replies, looking up at us, still grinning, happy with his gluey presents.

Clean-up occurs. Cotton towels are snatched up from the bathroom by Kirk. Chests are wiped down. Man-sap is removed from thighs and stomachs. Ginger has spew on his left cheek, and I rub it with a corner of towel. We're assiduous with our labor, laugh like college freshmen, and enjoy the task of clean-up almost as much as our previous round of tri-sex.

We sleep together after clean-up. Arms tangle together. Legs are pressed against sweaty thighs. Cocks touch during the early morning hours. Chests are fingered, lips brush together, and we become a twisting and turning puzzle on my bed, meshing together through the dawning hours, and enjoy each other while we sleep and dream.

Later this morning, Kirk and I decide to bang Milford again. Why not when he's willing (and capable) of taking on two dicks at the same time?

So Milford rides the cock-train for almost twenty-five minutes. He sways left and right, up and down, and a smile becomes bright-white on his face, showing his pleasure and delight. His firm erection bobs up and down and leaks pre-ooze out of its capped head. The pre-ejaculate flies in all directions and he yells within the apartment's confines, "Fuck me, you two! Ram your cocks into me!"

And so Kirk and I listen to the geek, and sexually satisfy him until all three of us become spent again, sticky, and covered in each other's perspiration.

Geek Log: August 5, 20 –

It is said that the meek will inherit the Earth, which I'm a firm believer in. Frankly, so will the geek, Milford Majeski. Something rather strange happens in the apartment on Chelsea Street. The three of us become boyfriends, processing an uber-liberal and – alternative relationship. We're not Mormon, but we certainly act like we are. It's an odd situation to speak the truth. I fuck around with Milford. He fucks around with Kirk. And Kirk fucks around with me. And sometimes we fuck around together, all three of us at the same time, banging like clumsy and twinkish XXX stars who just happen to be faithful boyfriends; an unbreakable trio of young men. We aren't meek by any means, but we're still geeky. Weird love entangles us together. A bizarre situation.

Will this arrangement last forever? I don't know. Neither do the biologist or ginger. Do I want it to last forever? Yes. But for now, I'll keep my two roommates for as long as they want me, and vice versa, of course. Who knows, the three of us maybe can make this work for decades, or even a lifetime.

Required note: Only time will tell.

Log End.

TEST TUBES AND LAB EXPERIMENTS
By Jay Starre

*Residing on English Bay in Vancouver, Canada,
Jay Starre is a writer and fitness trainer.
Contact: Jay Starre on Facebook.*

Professor Donahue was probably the worst teacher Dean ever had. Not that he was rude or incompetent; in fact he was polite and extremely knowledgeable about chemistry, which was his subject.

He was just too smart. He was reputed to be some kind of mutant genius and had invented a face cream for acne when he was just fifteen. He had then gone on to graduate from university at only twenty, and now he was teaching at that same university at only twenty-two. He was actually the same age as Dean.

Because he was so brilliant, he was unable to fathom the possibility his students couldn't always follow what he assumed was simple. Dean, who was lost most of the time, needed to study extra hard after class just to catch up.

It was that after-hours studying that got him into trouble. But the kind of trouble he got into turned out to be worth it, even if it was an undeniably kinky experience.

It happened when his young professor showed up to the lab without his contacts. Wearing oversized red-brimmed glasses instead, he looked totally different. Donahue was actually quite handsome, in a bland kind of way. Nondescript, actually. But on that day, with those bold unusual glasses, he looked more like who he really was, a geek genius. And totally intriguing! Dean was suddenly very turned on. He could not keep nasty thoughts from surfacing during their lab session the remainder of the evening.

So, he listened to the professor's long-winded lecture with even less attention than usual. At the end of the class, he realized he would have to study all the harder due to that lack of attention. With a boner throbbing in his jeans, he asked Donahue if he could remain after class and work on his own for a while. The Professor nodded politely as usual, but with no smile, no word of encouragement or any query as to whether he might need extra help. He really did suck as a teacher!

It was very late, the class ended at 11:00 pm that Wednesday evening, and there was practically zero chance anyone was going to come into the lab at that time. Since his roommate worked as one of the university cleaning staff for extra cash, Dean knew the custodians wouldn't get around to taking care of the labs until just before dawn.

He was alone; he was frustrated by the difficulty of his subject; and he was horny as hell. His thoughts

122

strayed from his books to his genius professor who had showed up with those strange red-framed glasses that were too big for his rather petite features and didn't match his conservative dark green lab coat and orange designer jeans. On top of all his other social inadequacies, he did not dress well.

After thirty minutes of attempted concentration, he surrendered. He was just too horny. He would have to jerk off. He went to the door and locked it, then decided to check out Donahue's desk drawers to see if he could find something that might work as lube. He knew the Prof was always working on some new cream since that was his claim to fame. The acne cream he had invented in his teens worked miracles, a fact Dean had discovered through his own use, and one reflected in the creamy pale and flawless complexion of the Prof himself.

Bonanza! Shoved behind boxes of paper clips and marking pens, he found something – a glass jar of what looked like lotion or cream.

The jar was labeled "Exp. Cream #398X." It seemed obvious it would be an experimental cream Donahue was currently working on. He opened it and took a sniff. It smelled great, a little like peppermint and lemon. It was so pale it was almost translucent, and when he dabbed a finger in it, it felt silky and slippery. Just what he was looking for.

He took it back to the lab table and pushed aside his books. The wall opposite was partially mirrored, and he grinned as he realized it would offer a great view of himself. He got up on the table, kicked off his shoes, then unsnapped his fly and pushed down his jeans. Off they came along with his underwear. He was naked from the waist down, now wearing only his T-shirt and the lab coat he still had on from their earlier lab session.

Laboratory tools were stored in a bin at the end of the table. He picked out one of the test tubes and chuckled to himself. Yep, it was smooth and long and shaped perfectly for a little ass-probing! Strong, too, as most of the lab implements were manufactured to withstand heat and pressure.

He dipped the cylindrical tube into the open container of cream. Then he lifted his legs and faced the mirror. Checking himself out, he couldn't help but be pleased with what he saw.

Half Mexican and half English, he had beautiful amber-brown skin. His golden ass was spread wide, smooth and round. His asshole, puckered and snug, was ready and waiting. Dean was a swimmer on the university team and had a long body with the supple muscles of his sport. He shaved his entire body, just like many of the competitive swimmers he knew. His dark brown hair was buzzed short across his round head, and he was smooth-shaven, too. His features stood out, a long narrow nose, full pink lips and luminous golden eyes. He stared at himself out of those bright eyes and grinned as he prepared his butt hole with a dollop of the slippery experimental cream smeared over the snug lips and clamped entrance.

It was immediately warm. Very warm! He couldn't wait to see how that test tube would feel inside. He placed the rounded end at the cream-coated entrance and slowly pressed. He usually had a tight hole, and it took a bit of time to open it up, but this time that was not the case. The tube slipped between his heated butt-lips like a warm knife in butter.

In fact, almost the entire tube slithered inside him. And it was so warm! He felt heat pulse in his gut and around the insides of his sphincter. He slid the tube out and stared at his hole. It twitched and pouted open. Yikes! It seemed to have grown totally relaxed. What was in that cream? He slid the tube back in, groaning with the warm pleasure of it. He pulled it out and stared again at how his hole remained wide open.

He was so intent on watching his hole react to the slippery tube and the cream that coated it, he was caught completely by surprise when a voice right beside him broke his concentration.

"I see you found my experimental cream."

"Fuck," he yelped as he turned his head to see Professor Donahue hovering over him. "You scared the shit out of me! Hell, sorry Prof, you really caught me unawares."

"No doubt. No doubt. I do have a key to the lab, of course." Donahue's voice was calm and polite as ever, even as a hand came out to press firmly on Dean's chest.

The message clear. Dean wasn't going to escape whatever it was the professor had in store for him. He would have to be disciplined for his nasty games with the Prof's personal property, his experimental cream!

125

Yet, Donahue didn't seem the least bit angry. He continued in his droll, even voice.

"No harm done. In fact, perhaps this is for the best. I have only experimented with this particular cream on myself and found it to have some unanticipated side effects. Another subject might not experience the same reaction. Shall we continue?"

"Uh, what is this stuff for? It sure is heating up my asshole, pardon me for being so crude, Prof."

"It is supposed to be a muscle relaxant, but it does elicit some heat, I have noted. It has worked wonders on my sore muscles after a vigorous workout in the gym."

"You work out in the gym?" Dean blurted out. That was a surprise.

"Yes. Regularly, of course. A disciplined mind requires a disciplined body. Now, first things first. As a basic precaution in any trial, we must immobilize the subject so that there is no opportunity for interference with the test."

"Uh, if you say so, Prof."

Dean wasn't entirely sure if he should let the young professor experiment on him, but he had to admit he was dying of curiosity. What did the geek genius have in mind? Was the quiet professor going to get nasty on him?

He sure the fuck hoped so!

Donahue certainly was quick and efficient, something Dean should have expected. It took him only a moment to search out some clear elastic tubing from a bin on the lab desk next to them.

Dean was already half naked and at a nod from the Prof, he understood he was to strip completely. His lab coat and T-shirt were discarded quickly, and he lay on the table totally naked, biting his lip and wondering what the hell was coming next.

"Let me know if you are uncomfortable," Donahue said quietly as he took hold of Dean's wrists and bound them with the tubing. Then, he pulled them back over his head and tied them to the back of the table on a hook embedded there, no doubt intended for other uses than this! A moment later, he was pulling Dean's ankle back toward his chest and to the side where he used more tubing to secure that foot to a similar hook at the side of the lab table. The other ankle was secured the same way.

He was actually comfortable, as weird as it seemed. The Prof just might have done something like this before!

"For this experiment, I believe it appropriate to test out the effects of my cream on the erogenous zones of the subject, and of course the subject would be yourself. Naturally, I admonish you to be completely honest with me. Tell me exactly what you are feeling as we go along. We can halt the experiment at any time."

The blond prof dipped two fingers from each hand into the open jar of experimental cream and then proceeded to use his fingers to coat both Dean's butt-hole and his cock-head with the slick substance. Even though he claimed this was a clinical experiment, the professor's fingers rubbed all over Dean's pouting butt lips and onto the head of his cock very slowly and sensually, much more so than seemed necessary. He looked up from his work and into Dean's eyes as he slowly began to probe his asshole with the two fingers stroking his twitching butt hole.

Even though his fingers weren't exactly proving clinical, his voice still maintained its quiet deliberation when he spoke. "Your hole seems very relaxed. Is it always this relaxed?" The fingers slithered past his quaking butt lips and tunneled deep into him. He groaned and squirmed slightly, feebly attempting to maintain a bit of composure to match Donahue's. But that was totally impossible.

"No way am I usually so relaxed! It feels really warm in there. And really good, too," he admitted with a gasp.

"Interesting. Let's try something else."

Dean was very disappointed when the two fingers withdrew. His hole went into little heated spasms that felt really good, too, before he was distracted by Donahue as he scooped out more of the translucent cream and proceeded to rub it onto Dean's nipples. He gazed down into Dean's eyes as he did, very intently – but still not smiling.

"And how does this feel?"

"Amazing! Fucking amazing, I have to admit!"

"Very good. Let's try somewhere else." A moment later he was massaging some of the cream onto Dean's plump balls.

He spoke in a matter-of-fact and clinical manner. "How does that feel?"

"Good!"

"Can you be more specific please?"

"Hot. It throbs. It makes me want to rub my balls, and rub my cock, and put something up my fucking asshole," he grunted out.

By now he was really squirming, and it was probably a good thing Donahue had secured him or he would have done all those things to himself and interfered with the prof's little experiment.

"Let's put something up your ass, then, and see if that satisfies it."

He picked out a glass flask from the tool bin and coated it with some of the experimental cream. The cylindrical tube had a round bulb at one end, and Donahue placed it down between Dean's splayed thighs against his ass crack. Staring down at himself, the bound student noticed that his cock had grown huge. Even though the shaft hadn't been coated with the cream, it seemed to have swollen up considerably, and his cock head was a giant purple knob! It leaked pre-cum, too, adding to its glistening sheen.

Donahue slid the big rounded end of the glass flask all over his coated butt lips, then planted it at dead center and applied steady pressure. It popped inside and Dean groaned. The prof slowly pushed it deeper, and deeper, then he just as slowly pulled it back out, taking extra time to hold it just within the quaking sphincter before popping it out.

He scooped out more of the cream and used his fingers again to probe deep into Dean's hole. "Yes, you are even more relaxed now. Let's see if we can get more inside you."

He slipped the bulbed flask back inside and buried it deep, then pulled it right back out with a pop. Next, he put three fingers in the gaping hole. He looked up into Dean's eyes as he slowly twisted them in circles.

"And how does that feel?

"Awesome. Fucking awesome!"

"Can you take more?"

"Try me!"

Donahue nodded, then slowly pushed a fourth finger inside. Dean grunted loudly and heaved upward on the table, not to get away from the fingers, but to get them even deeper inside. His asshole felt like a bottomless pit!

"Very interesting, Dean. The ramifications of these obvious side effects could be important. I think we should try some fucking. Are you comfortable with that?"

"Uh, sure."

Donahue stripped down quickly, and entirely naked, climbed up onto the lab table and crouched over Dean's face. "It would be best if you could warm me up first. I am not quite as prepared as you for the next step."

Dean was dying to find out what that next step would be. Who would fuck who? But for now, he was faced with a gorgeous ass and cock to look after.

Donahue's cock dangled down over Dean's face. It was surprisingly thick and long considering the relatively small stature of its owner. It was also swollen up into an obvious hard-on, so it was apparent the prof was getting turned on by the proceedings.

His crack was as enticing as his big cock. It was smooth and deep between two very round and full butt cheeks. Ivory pale, the skin was totally hairless. In the center, the flushed pink hole pouted outward as he crouched directly over the Dean's face.

"Go ahead. Lick my ass and crotch. Lick all over, including the hole and my balls. Once you've got me really wet, then I'll employ some of the cream on my erogenous zones."

That beautiful ass descended and Dean opened his mouth and stuck out his tongue. The crack slid across his open mouth and nose, and he inhaled clean, manly ass and hole as his tongue slithered all along it. He tickled the clenched butt lips with the tip of his tongue and was rewarded by a twitching response. He dared more and probed with his tongue. Donahue's hole opened slightly as he pressed downward to nearly smother Dean.

He rose after a moment and moved slightly backwards so that the head of his cock grazed Dean's lips. The student took the hint and began to suck on it. The plump crown slithered into his mouth and pushed toward his tonsils as Donahue slowly fucked his mouth.

The blond prof alternated between fucking Dean's mouth with that thick cock and rubbing his tempting asshole over his nose and mouth. At the same time, he was leaning forward enough to continue experimenting on the student's wide open ass. He popped the cream-coated flask in and out of Dean's hole in a steady and maddening rhythm.

"I believe we can move on now," Donahue finally said. This time, Dean thought he detected a bit of a quaver in the professor's voice.

He moved forward to squat over Dean's rearing cock, facing the mirror and offering the bound student a perfect view of his back and ass. Donahue was slim, but had surprisingly broad and well-muscled shoulders. He apparently wasn't lying when he claimed he worked out regularly. His back tapered down to a very narrow waist and those full, ivory-pale butt cheeks.

He reached back and coated his ass crack with some of the cream, paying particular attention to the spit-wet and slightly gaping butt lips Dean had just been licking. Then he took hold of Dean's cock and placed the head against the entrance to his well-coated hole.

The swollen knob, purple and twitching, looked enormous. It seemed like it would take some effort to force it between those snug butt lips. But with amazing ease, it slipped inside and then was completely swallowed up as the blond prof sat down on him.

"Oh my fucking god! It is so hot in there! It feels like my cock has been swallowed by a volcano," he blurted out.

"It is very hot, I agree. Your cock is extremely warm inside me, definitely. I would guess at least a few degrees above normal body temperature."

Donahue began to hump Dean with slow, thorough strokes, rising and falling in a steady rhythm that had the student alternately yelping and moaning. Normally, he would have shot his load by now with all that hot and steamy action, but for some reason he was able to hold back. He realized it might be a side effect of the cream. He imagined it was something Donahue would want to know.

"I feel like I can hold off from coming, even though it feels like I should. Maybe it's the cream," he reported dutifully, although he could barely speak as he watched that awesome ass rising and falling over his lap and his own swollen cock disappear and reappear, glistening with the silky experimental cream.

"Interesting. I feel we should test out that hypothesis."

Dean wasn't sure what he meant by that, until Donahue pivoted around with cock still planted in his steamy butt-hole and faced him. The professor's own cock was stiff and leaking pre-cum copiously.

Donahue then coated his stiff cock with more of the cream, all over the rigid shank and around the bulbous crown. It glistened with a sheen of slick lubricant and twitched wildy once he let go of it.

"Fuck me harder. I want you to make me come without me even touching my cock. I want to see if I can come from just the sensation of the cream on my cock and on your cock inside my ass. Fuck me really hard. Really hard."

His gaze was intense as once more he began to ride Dean's thrusting rod.

"I believe it is time to release you," Donahue said between slight gasps. He reached out and did so, as quickly and efficiently as he had tied him up in the first place, while still riding his cock!

"Put your fingers in my ass, too. I am feeling really relaxed, just as you have been. Let's see how stretched we can get me."

Music to Dean's ears, he reached around the squatting prof and grabbed hold of his rising and falling butt cheeks. For their large size, they were extremely firm! He slipped his fingers into the crack to find it liberally coated with the cream. He had put much more on himself than he had on Dean.

With amazing ease, two of Dean's fingers slipped into Donahue hole beside his cock.

"My fingers feel great inside you! You really are relaxed Prof!"

"Excellent. I do feel really relaxed." His voice really quavered now!

As he thrust two of his fingers in deep to feel his cock slither and slide, Dean could tell Donahue was getting close to blowing. Even though he continued staring directly into Dean's eyes from behind those oversized red-framed glasses, with his neatly trimmed and parted hair, he was still totally naked and riding a hard cock for all he was worth. His mouth was open, and he was beginning to pant, and then he let out a really loud grunt.

He shot. His cum sprayed in an arc that hit Dean's forehead and hair and even beyond. It was amazing!

A few moments of gasping silence followed before the professor rose off Dean's lap to climb off the table and stand beside him. Dean believed their little scientific trial might be over at that point.

"Thank you. That felt quite spectacular. Now it's your turn."

"Oh, sure. To finish off the experiment, I guess."

"Well, yes. But also, it would not be considerate of me to leave you unsatisfied. You have been very cooperative and very helpful."

That was something Dean hadn't expected. He found himself beginning to actually like the mad scientist. He liked him even more once he began to finger Dean's ass, first with one finger, then two and three, and ever so slowly and deeply. At the same time Donahue massaged cream all over his throbbing cock. Dean groaned and squirmed and totally let go, not caring if he looked like a total slut in heat. All the while Donahue gazed at him intently from behind those red-framed glasses and worked his cock and hole to their limits, finally forcing him to shoot as wild a load as the prof had earlier.

As they cleaned up with wet cloths, each helping the other, and in no particular rush to get it over and done with, Dean began to suspect Donahue was lonely and wanted to have a friend. At least he wanted to think so. His suspicion seemed justified a moment later.

Still naked, the blond prof asked Dean if he would be willing to continue their experiments over the next few weeks. "Just to make sure there are no effects we have overlooked," he reasoned.

Hell yeah, he wanted to shout. He agreed immediately.

The geeky professor was not exactly a barrel of laughs, or barely even a bit charming, but he was polite, and had proved himself to be considerate, which was more than could be said for a lot of people.

Dean decided right then and there his new mission in life would be to make the serious professor smile. And have one hell of a lot of kinky fun in the process!

PORN TO BE WILD
By Logan Zachary

Logan Zachary is a bear author of more than 100 short erotica stories and several books. He lives in Minneapolis. www.loganzacharydicklit.com and loganzachary2002@yahoo.com.

My roommate would slink into our dorm room at all hours of the day and night. He smelled funny, like formaldehyde or some other chemical. His long hair was greasy and unkempt. His white lab coat was wrinkled and stained, smelling like nothing I could explain. His pocket protector held strange tools in it.

I didn't see him eat at the cafeteria or invite friends over to our room to study. I felt sorry for him from his thick, Coke bottle glasses that distorted his eyes and covered most of his face to his Goodwill clothes that made him look as if he stepped out of the 1950s.

Strange symbols covered every inch of the pages in Gavin Holland's notebooks. My calculus homework looked as if a preschooler had filled it out compared to his writings. My parents asked how I was getting along with my roommate, and I wasn't sure what to say. Great, since we never had a conflict. Bad, since we never talked, never saw each other, or ever interacted.

I know I could fly my own freak flag if I wanted to: Rainbow flag, Rainbow jock, butt plug, nipple clamps. Well, maybe not nipple clamps. Ouch.

I tossed my back pack on my upper bunk and looked down at Gavin's unmade, empty bed. A plain brown bag was under his pillow. I looked back at the door. He never came home in the daylight flashed through my mind, and a chill settled over me. I know. I've seen way too many horror movies, and shows like *Desperate Housewives* have made it okay to snoop in other people's things. So, I rolled back the folded paper flap and peaked inside: *Naked Frat Boys*, *Horny Jocks*, and *Hairy Holes*.

So Gavin was gay, too. But what was he doing? Did he work in a meth lab? Maybe he was just a TA in the chem. Or bio lab. But how many students got that gig?

Then I remembered what he looked like.

He was a geek. He would be perfect for that job. I wanted to look inside the magazines, but I didn't want to get a raging hard on or have him walk in on me. I shoved his porn back into the bag and slipped it back under his pillow. Just as I did. I heard a key slip into the lock, and the dorm room door opened.

I reached up into my bunk and opened my back pack. I pulled out a book and pretended to be looking for something else. "Hey," I called over my shoulder.

"Hey," Gavin said, and waited for me to move from his bed. His gaze nervously looked down to his pillow, which I saw in the reflection of the window.

Could he tell I moved it? I pretended to climb up on to my bunk and partially stepped on his bed and made the mattress shift. "Sorry, I'm very clumsy today. I really need to hit the shower."

As soon as I moved over to my chest of drawers, Gavin dove for his bed and covered his pillows with his body.

"Any plans for the weekend?" I asked, as I opened a drawer and pulled out clean underwear and socks.

Gavin stared at me as I pulled them out and set them down. I bent to the bottom drawer and pulled out a towel. I could feel the heat of his eyes on my ass. Well, if he wanted to see something …

Kicking off my shoes, I sat down to pull off my socks. I tossed them into my laundry bag. I peeled off my shirt and undid my pants.

"How was your week? I'm so glad it's Friday and mine's over."

I swear drool pooled at the corner of his mouth as he watched me strip. I was a good looking guy. Hairy chest, six pack abs, long muscular hairy legs and arms. I stepped out of my jeans and stood there in my tighty whities. I could feel my cock start to swell in the thin cotton. I turned around and bent over, knowing how the briefs rode deep into my crack and hugged my cheeks.

I felt sorry for him and wanted him to get something. I debated if I should take off my underwear and before I could change my mind. I pushed them down and bared my hairy ass. I spread my legs to reveal my pink pucker and felt my balls dangle back and forth. My cock sprang to full length and started to ooze.

You are such a fucking tease, I told myself. I wrapped the towel around my waist and said, "Did you need a shower? Get ready for the weekend?" All I could do was offer. Make him feel welcome.

His hands covered his groin, and he looked as if he was in pain.

"I can wait if you want."

"Nah," he grunted.

"Okay." I padded bare foot to the door and left the room.

As I entered the bathroom, I realized I didn't have my room key, my underwear, socks, soap or shampoo. "Crap." Too late now. I jumped into a stall and took the towel off. A bottle of shampoo sat on the shelf. My lucky day. I turned on the hot water and let it washed me clean. It relaxed my muscles but did little for my erection. After drying off, I headed back to our room. The door was ajar, and as I opened the door, Gavin was still in his bed.

I had to do it. I am evil. I headed to my bunk and reached into my book bag. The damp towel clung to my body, and my cock was still rock hard inside. I pulled myself up onto my bed, and my towel fell off.

Crap.

That wasn't part of my plan. I lay on my belly with my stiff dick against the bed, and my bare ass up in the air. I held perfectly still and waited.

"Reed, are you coming down?" Gavin asked.

"I think I'm a little under dressed."

"That is a problem."

Did he know I had been playing him? Teasing him? Or not?

I think this was the first time we had been in the room together for more than five minutes where both of us were awake.

"You can come down. I don't mind."

Was he pimping me? He couldn't. He was a geek. They didn't have a sense of humor, or did they?

"I have a little problem right now," I said, as I adjusted my hard-on.

"It didn't look that little to me."

He moved on the bunk beneath me, and I heard the mattress springs creek as he got off of it. He rolled out of the bed and picked up my damp towel.

I pulled my blanket to cover my ass and then looked to see his back was to me as he reached backward to hand me the discarded towel.

"You looked at my magazines, didn't you?"

"I ... I ..."

"They were out of order. It's fine if you looked at them."

"I didn't have the chance open them." I didn't reach for my towel. I watched as he waved his arm back and forth offering it to me.

His head turned to give a side glance over his shoulder to see where I was and turn away if I was exposed.

I leaned on my elbows and flexed my butt cheeks under the blanket. "It's fine if you want to look, too. We are roommates after all. How can we live together in such close quarters and never see each other?"

Gavin turned and approached the bed. His gaze scanned over my shoulders, down my back and hovered over the crest of my hairy ass, then went down my long legs. His hand placed the damp towel at my feet.

"I touched your stuff. I feel it's only fair to let you touch my stuff." I moved and the blanket pulled back and uncovered part of my ass. I didn't know if he would bolt or attack. I held my breath and waited.

Carefully, his hand caressed my ankle and slowly made its way up my hairy calf. It dipped at my knee and stalled out for a moment before he switched his hand position. His thumb moved over to ride up between my legs and higher into my butt crack. His thumb tickled the hair on my sack and then traced along my damp crease.

I moaned, enjoying his finger as it traced a design on my backside. I closed my eyes and lay down, spreading my legs wider for him.

His other hand reached over, and then he used both hands to grab my ass and kneaded my gluts.

I arched my back, pushing my dick into my mattress, and when my ass rose up, I pressed my butt into his hands.

One of his fingertips brushed against my tender pucker, and I thought I was going to shoot my load as he pressed on it.

"You like that?" he asked, as he stepped onto his bed. He climbed onto my bunk and moved between my legs. A wet, warm tongue licked between my cheeks and over the pink pucker.

I grabbed onto my blanket and held on for dear life.

He licked in circles, and then over the whole hairy hole only to explore deeper and deeper, seeking entry.

I pushed back against his mouth and relaxed my ass.

145

He slipped in deeper and kissed me with pressure.

I always considered myself a top, but if he could do this … He could do this and anything he wanted to my ass.

His hands worked on his pants, and he broke the seal on my butt with a pop and rose up to release himself.

I felt a heavy, fleshy weight flop on my leg, and I looked back.

He had the biggest dick I had ever seen. It snaked out of his pants and grew as it neared my wet and waiting ass.

He stroked the fat uncut head along my leg toward my hairy crease.

I was about to protest when he pulled out a rubber and a bottle of lube. He unrolled the condom and slathered his massive dick with the oil. He greased my butt and teased my hole. He guided his fat mushroom head to the opening and pulled back on my hips, doggie style.

I rose up and was painlessly impaled on his dick. As soon as he was all the way in, his hands grabbed my erection and lubed me up. Slowly, he stroked me as my balls swung back and forth. I pressed back on him and rode his cock as his hand sent waves of pleasure over my body. His hands were skilled.

Harder, faster, deeper, we moved. I couldn't stop. I wanted it, now. Sweat ran down my forehead and burned my eyes, but I didn't care. The joy flowed over our bodies as they became one.

Gavin pulled out of me, and my ass cried for more. He tapped my shoulder and motioned for me to roll over onto my back.

I dropped and rolled over, ankles in the air so fast; he didn't have enough time to take off his shirt. I arched my back and spread my legs wide.

His huge cock slipped in easily and went even deeper with this new angle. He was able to play with my balls and cock as he humped.

Slam!

Slam!

Slam!

His body plunged into mine, and he made bliss erupt all over me. I grabbed my ankles and held tight as my toes curled and my legs tightened to get him in deeper and harder. His balls slapped my ass and stung where they hit, but the pain turned all into pleasure.

How could this unassuming guy be such a talented lover? Why had I been so wrong about him?

Gavin reached forward and pinched a nipple. His hand caressed my pec. He took his glasses off and

147

slicked his hair back, before he pulled me up. His mouth descended on mine and electricity flowed through my body. His kiss sent a shock down to my cock, and I exploded in his hand.

Cum flowed out of his fist and covered my chest. He thrust into me a few more times as his grunting became louder and louder. His tongue entered my mouth, and I felt a gush of heat fill my butt. Spasm after spasm hit my body as he hammered into me. He continued to jack my dick and milked out another wave of cum.

I fell back on the bed exhausted.

He landed on top of me, sweat and semen squishing between us, holding us together. His cock was still buried deep inside me.

As I opened my eyes, I saw how handsome he was. His wild hair and thick glasses hid the true hunk inside. I pushed the lock of hair back from his face and held his head in my hands. "You are amazing." I kissed him, long deep and passionately.

Gavin returned my kiss, thrusting his still hard cock deeper into me as his tongue entered my mouth.

"I didn't know you would even talk to me, let alone … I thought you were just a dumb jock looking for his next piece of tail."

I squeezed his ass. "This is the best tail I've ever seen."

Gavin kissed me, light and carefree. He was happy and relaxed. He popped out of me and rolled over to lie next to me.

I wrapped my arm around him and held him close.

"You're all sweaty and sticky again," he said as he cuddled next to me.

"Then maybe you should shower with me, next time." I hugged him closer, and he knew I meant it. "So what do you do? I never see you. Have I offended you, and you stay away from our room because of me?"

Gavin laughed and slapped my chest. "No. I'm in the lab working. It's part of my work study, and it pays for my tuition."

"I could use a gig like that. My scholarship is almost gone."

"You could help me collect samples." Gavin said as he rose onto his elbow and looked down at me. He squinted, since his glasses were still off, but his beautiful blue eyes glowed.

# # # # #

After hitting the showers, I took Gavin to my stylist, and he got his hair cut.

Wow, is all I can say.

We had supper at the mall, stopped into the Vision Center for contact lens, and ran through a few stores for a few new shirts and pants. The rest of the weekend, Gavin and I spent in bed.

Monday morning dawned with a new stud, I mean, a new student on campus, and he was my friend. When my classes were over, I met Gavin at the biology lab. He was waiting for me with his lab coat worn over his new clothes.

Dr. Holland was working in his office when we walked in. He rose and extended his hand. "Reed, so you're the Dr. Frankenstein roommate that made a new man out of my Gavin, nice to finally meet you."

I shook his hand and sat down in the chair he motioned to.

Gavin hung in the doorway, and Dr. Holland motioned for him to stay. He sat next to me in the other chair.

"Gavin said you need a job, and we could use all the help we can get for our project. I'm sure he hasn't said anything about it. He wanted me to explain." Dr. Holland looked at Gavin, and he nodded.

Dr. Holland looked over at me and said, "What we're working on is of a sensitive nature and so far, only a few select people know what we are working on. Gavin knows a little but not everything, and he is doing the collecting, so it's important he understands what the process is and what we are trying to achieve."

I leaned forward and turned my head to the side to hear better. My heart rate was increasing, and I was getting a little concerned. I took Bio 101 three years ago as a freshman, but that was the only science class I needed. I swallowed hard, worried I didn't have what it took.

Dr. Holland looked down at my hands and smiled. "You have nice big, muscular hands that are soft. Good."

I looked at my hands and then over at Gavin's. They looked similar.

Dr. Holland smiled. "I know what happened over the weekend, and that makes this all the easier to discuss."

Gavin's face flushed red. "He suspected something happened after my looks changed."

Then the realization hit me. Gavin Holland. Dr. Holland.

"I know my son is gay. I knew it before he did, and when I asked him to help with my experiment, he actually enjoyed it. Now, with that being said, I don't want this job to come between you, two."

Gavin reached over and grabbed my hand and squeezed. "Dad, we're not getting married."

"I know, but this job may cause hard feelings between you, two."

Gavin laughed. "You said hard …" and he couldn't go on.

Dr. Holland raised his hand and looked at me, trying not to laugh. "What Gavin is being so juvenile about is that we collect samples here. Semen samples, by hand." He looked down at my hand. "Your hand."

I forced myself not to pull my hand back.

"You can add your semen to the project. I hope you horny boys will do, it'll help a lot, but the best way to explain the experiment is to show you." Dr. Holland rose to and walked out of the office.

Gavin and I followed.

I could tell Gavin was nervous. Maybe he was having second thoughts about having me help.

Dr. Holland opened a door, and we entered a long room with a wall of one way mirrors. In each treatment room, a naked college student lay on his back as another person in a lab coat jacked him off. There was a long suction tube that was used to collect the load after the guy came.

I turned to Gavin and looked at his stained lab coat.

"That's mustard, mayo, and ketchup, no body fluids. Honest." He crossed his heart.

"So you want me to jack off guys and collect their spunk?"

Gavin backed up a step.

Dr. Holland's brow furrowed, and said, "Basically, yes. Will that be a problem for you?"

"Hell no. Sign me up."

Gavin hugged me, and it was my turn to blush.

"I can see why you like him," Dr. Holland said with a wink to his son.

I was fit for my lab coat, and Gavin and his dad trained me on how to use the suction device. It was nerve racking to walk into the first room and see the handsome college student with a raging hard-on. I entered with a surgical cap, goggles, and a mask over my mouth, which made me unrecognizable.

I donned rubber gloves and poured some lube into my hands and started to stroke his penis. At my touch, his cock grew and swelled.

Do I talk to him? Do I just jack him of? What if he needs more help? Could I stick my finger up his ass to stimulate his prostate gland? So many crazy questions ran through my mind, and all of sudden his dick exploded in my hand. I grabbed the wand and sucked the juicy load up and made him ooze a little more as I ran the collection device over the head of his cock.

153

I looked up into the mirror, wondering if the technique was proper and would work for this sample. I was warned if the semen was handled improperly, it would be discarded, and money for the student would come – ha ha – out of my pocket/paycheck.

He smiled as I handed him a wet cloth, and he washed the lube from his dick and balls. As he stood and bent over, his amazing ass winked at me, and I was instantly hard.

This was going to be a hard job.

I headed back to the lab to make sure all went well, and Dr. Holland shook his finger at me.

"You need to pay attention. We can't use the sample if it's contaminated."

My face flushed as I bit my lower lip. "I was worried I was doing it all wrong and bamm, he came."

"That's why there's the green light in the corner, so you know you're doing fine. Just relax, have fun, enjoy and give them what they need."

My dick jumped in my jeans and some pre-cum oozed out into my briefs. I knew my laundry would double working at this job, but the money and bene's were great.

Gavin rubbed my shoulder. "You did great. Just relax and have fun. Don't think of it as a job. Enjoy each dick." He kissed me and said, "But just not as much as you enjoy mine."

I headed back to the sample room and almost crapped my pants.

Rob "The Clinger" Clingington was pulling off his pants and stood there in his stained jock strap. His huge cock stretched the elastic pouch as far as it could go. The hair from his balls stuck out of the holes and poured out the sides of the cup. His tight ass was framed in the back straps, highlighting it in the best light possible.

"I enjoy some gentle ball play and a finger in my ass," The Clinger said. "They help me come."

I stepped back.

"I'm not gay. It just speeds up the process, honest." He slipped the jock off, and his cock swelled to full size.

I ... I ... and then I remembered, he couldn't recognize me. I could play with that amazing cock and ass, and ... and ...

I jumped forward, slammed the door shut and fumbled to get my gloves on. I could hear Gavin's laughter in my mind as I tried to calm myself down. I used both hands to cradle his balls and lube up his dick. I needed more lube to cover his business.

As the second coating of lube covered my finger, I slipped it under his heavy sack and searched for his hairy hole. My finger touched the moist opening and pressed. It was tight and resisted. I circled the lube around and around. Pushing it in and trying to go deeper, as I stroked his cock. My fingers had a hard time wrapping around his shaft and widened even more over the fat head.

The scent of his sweat from practice and cut grass rose from his footballer's body. He rocked his hips and helped my hands stimulate the right nerves. Pre-cum started to ooze out of his cock and mix with the lube.

I rolled his balls with my thumb and drilled in deeper into his amazing ass.

"Deeper, deeper," he moaned.

I pushed in harder and harder. His ass was wet and warm, so tight and perfect, my own dick hurt in my scrubs. I jacked and jacked as I fingered his butt.

"Put another one in," he asked.

My middle finger entered him as my index finger slipped back in.

"Oh yeah, give it to me."

I worked on his cock for a while, and he still oozed pre-cum, but no orgasm.

His hand slapped at me. "Use your cock. Fuck me, fuck me hard."

The green light came in one of the corners, and I knew that meant I could.

I pulled out of his ass, untied my scrubs and let them drop to the floor. I shoved my wet underwear down and slammed into his tight ass.

Oh, yes. He was so fucking hot. I stroked his dick as I plunged into him and my rhythm sped up. I pulled his muscular legs over my shoulders and gained full penetration with my dick. My balls slammed against his ass, and I used both hands to work his cock.

The pleasure rose in my balls, and I knew I didn't have long before I shot my load. I jacked harder and harder, making his balls rise up and drop back on my shaft as I entered him.

He rode on my dick and moaned and groaned. "Yes, yes. Harder, HARDER!" he screamed as the biggest explosion erupted from his cock.

My hand grabbed the wand and caught his huge load. I continued to slam into his ass, hitting his prostate gland and forcing another orgasm out of his balls.

"YES!!!" he howled for the longest time as I vacuumed his dick. As the last drop slurped in, I pulled out of his ass and came into the wand's head. My juices flowed in wave after wave. One hand still worked his cock as the other sucked my sack empty.

A pearl of his cum pooled at the end of his dick, and I had to taste him. I pulled up the mask and leaned forward to lick that drip of his tip. Sweet ambrosia, but not as sweet as Gavin's.

Both loads were captured, and I felt great.

The Clinger brought his legs down and lay there huffing and puffing.

I put my tools away, cock and collector, and handed him a warm, wet washcloth.

"Wipe me clean," he demanded.

Another chance to play with his junk?

Hell yes. I love my job.

I wiped his lemon sized balls and dug underneath to clean his hairy hole. As his bottom was washed, I swirled along his girth and over the massive head. I took a few extra swipes, just for my pleasure and blew on him to dry his business.

He grabbed his ankles and spread his cheeks wide. His pink pucker shined as I blew on it. My tongue wanted to taste him, but I prayed there would a next time.

Once dry, he slowly rose and pulled on his pants. His jock lay on the floor under the table.

I bent to pick it up. As I handed it to him, he said, "Keep it. I have more."

After he left, I slipped the damp jock into a zip lock bag and put it in my pocket. The item burned as it touched my skin.

The door opened, and my Analytical Geometry professor entered.

I really love my job.

# # # # #

Despite my heavy class load, I was able to log almost forty hours a week in the lab. The paycheck was nice, but the time with Gavin was even better. No matter how handsome or hung the guy was that I milked, Gavin held my heart.

Our dorm room was no longer a cold sterile place, it was warm and inviting. New sheets, pillows, and a thick comforter made snuggling in bed so much more fun in the cold room on winter days.

# # # # #

As we closed up the lab one late Friday night, I asked Gavin, "What does your Dad do with all the semen?"

Gavin gave me the strangest look and paused. "You know, I don't know."

"Do you know where it goes?" I asked.

"No."

I followed Gavin to the side door and walked up the metal stairs to the second floor. A system of tubes that looked like an octopus came up from the treatment rooms and converged into the central processing center. A large pipe rose from the center and made a ninety degree angle at the ceiling. The pipe ran across the beam and exited to the next chamber.

Gavin pulled on the door and found it locked.

I pointed at the keypad and cardkey slit before sliding my access card down the shute.

ACCESS DENIED.

Gavin slid his card key through the slot. The lights spun and spun, trying to process his card, and they finally turned green.

ACCESS ALLOWED.

The magnetic lock clicked, and there was a rush of gases as the air tight chamber opened with a hiss.

I looked at him in shock. Did we need respirators?

The door swung open, and we peered in.

A huge glass tank stood in the center of the dark room, and a blue light came from inside. The glow made the liquid swirl and move as if it were a living mass, creamy white and shiny, shimmering bright in the strange light. Then I realized it was a black light.

I looked at the ceiling and pointed at the tube running across the beam and dropping down into the glass tank.

"It's filled with semen!" Gavin gasped.

I moved closer to look deeper into the tank.

It towered over me. It must have been at least ten feet tall, four feet wide and deep.

Something moved in the center of the tank.

"Did you see that?" I asked.

Gavin smiled at me. "You're just trying to scare me," he said as he came to stand next to me and took my hand. "What do you think …?"

And a hand brushed up against the inside of the tank.

We both jumped back.

The palm pressed against the glass and slid up and down, fingers on one hand flexing and extending, and then a second hand appeared.

"What is your dad working on?" I asked as we retreated to the door. My back came in contact with a body, and I squealed in surprise.

Dr. Holland blocked our exit.

161

"Da ... Dad what's up?" Gavin asked.

Dr. Holland raised his hands and smiled. "So you've found out my secret experiment."

"What are you doing?" I asked.

"Semen is the perfect media to grow a man. There is fructose for an energy supply, proteolytic enzymes to decrease inflammation, fluids for lubrication, and the seminal plasma provides both a nutrient base and a protective medium to protect from a hostile environment."

"Protect what, Dad?" Gavin asked. He wrapped his arm around me.

I understood half of what he talked about from my Bio 101 class, but the rest was over my head.

Gavin looked at his Dad. "What are you saying? You haven't gone all Dr. Frankenstein on me?"

"Just imagine if we could turn on all of the genes of the egg and sperm cells, think of what we could do with replacing damaged organs. No more dialysis, lung cancer, any cancer, healthy hearts, no more Alzheimer's, Parkinson's, MS, ALS, all diseases gone." Dr. Holland took a step toward us.

We backed up and stood next to the tank.

Whatever was inside, wanted out. It thumped and bumped on the glass, a hollow sound like someone knocking on glass blocks echoed in the room. The silhouette of a man pressed against the glass, a hairy chest, flat pale abs, a big penis, and two long, hairy muscular legs.

"Perfect timing." Dr. Holland's eyes lit up.

I was worried Dr. Holland would shriek, it's alive; it's alive!

He walked behind the tank and climbed up the metal stairs. He opened the top and slid the lid off. Come dripped from the cap and splattered on the floor. The room smelled of sex and semen, man and sweat. Dr. Holland put on rubber gloves and reached into the glowing, swirling goo. A slimy, semen covered arm grabbed onto him and pulled.

The old doc was ready and leaned back assisting the form to climb out of the slippery tank.

The emerging man gasped and coughed as he spat out the semen in his mouth. He flopped onto the walkway with the doctor and collapsed on weak legs.

Dr. Holland picked up the nozzle of the hose attached to the stairway. He turned it on and rinsed the naked man off. He carefully cleaned the man, washing the goo and water down the floor drain.

Gavin and I stood in mock horror at a beautiful blond man sat on the steps. Pink lines ran all over his body, but they were smooth and faint. Not like the thick, black stitching seen in the horror movies. He towered over seven feet tall, powerful legs and arms, rippling with muscles, an even pelt of hair covered flat abs, bulging pecs, a narrow waist, and a monstrous penis.

As Dr. Holland finished, he turned off the water and reached down. He helped the man to his feet and escorted him down the steps. The man's bare feet struggled on the hard metal.

"Gavin, grab that lab coat." He pointed to the row of coats on the wall.

Gavin left my side and did his father's bidding.

I watched as the perfect man walked toward me. Toned athlete meets fashion model stood pale and shivering. His penis swung back and forth as he neared. His deep blue eyes looked at me and smiled.

"Boys meet Adam. Adam meet the boys. Adam needs a place to crash for the weekend, and I hope you can … take good care of him," Dr. Holland said.

Adam reached for me and grabbed my chest. His wet hand squeezed my pec and nodded.

Gavin came around his father and brought the lab coat over Adam's shoulders. He helped Adam get his arms into the holes, and I was sad to see his god's body disappear under the coat.

Adam's hand went down my arm and grabbed my wrist. He pulled my hand into the lab coat's opening and rubbed my hand on his quickly arising cock.

My fingers instantly wrapped around his swelling girth and started to gently stroke.

His penis was still damp and slid easily in my hand. His skin was soft and tender like a new born. He groaned with increasing passion as I sped up.

"Gavin, Reed, no sex for twenty-four hours." His father ordered as I continued to jack him off.

"A ... A...." Adam said as he arched his back and shot a huge load across the floor and the majority landed on Dr. Holland's shoe.

He frowned at me. "He's a newborn teenager. His hormones will be raging as will his libido."

I shrugged as I tried to pull my hand from Adam's grasp. "He made me do it," I said.

Adam shook his head and smiled.

"Liar," he said, as I stroked him a few more times on his overly sensitive dick, before I let go.

Adam let go of my hand immediately and hunched forward, pulling his overly sensitive organ away from my touch.

My hand was covered in his cum. I moved over to the workbench to get a tissue.

"There are boots over there, too," Dr. Holland said to me as I threw away the glob.

I headed over toward the door and bent over to pick the boots up.

The three men followed close behind me, and Adam grabbed my ass before I could stand up straight.

Dr. Holland let Gavin take over holding Adam up, but we could see Adam's strength was quickly returning. Dr. Holland pulled his cell phone out of his pocket and dialed a number. "Charles, can you bring the car around to the back of the lab. The boys are ready to head back to the dorm."

I knelt and helped Adam get his feet into the boots. I looked up at Dr. Holland. "How did you know we'd go looking in your secret lab?"

Dr. Holland chuckled to himself. "Two horny boys collecting semen, come on. I'm surprised it took you this long. Well, have a fun weekend." And he headed out the lab's door.

"Wait. We have to babysit him for the weekend?" Gavin asked.

"I'm sure you'll find something to do." Dr. Holland paused and reached into his wallet, pulled out a credit card, and tossed it to me. "The weekend's on me. Enjoy."

We guided Adam to the waiting car and started one hell of a wild weekend.

Dr. Holland called after us, "And boys, no porn."

SQUARE BEAR
By Landon Dixon

Dixon's writing credits include many, many magazines, anthologies, and the short story collections Hot Tales of Gay Lust 1, 2, and 3.

"I've been looking over these deductions, Mr. Purman, and ... well, something doesn't seem right."

He looked up from the payroll register lying open in his lap, his metal-framed glasses flashing in the bright afternoon sun streaming in through the window in back of me. It was one of my little tricks – to shine the spotlight on my interrogator. It wasn't working.

"This pension deduction for Theo Vandemeer, for example ..." he said, holding the register up toward me.

I leaned back in my chair and crossed my legs, folded my hands together. Moving farther away from the incriminating accounting ledger, not closer. "Those calculations are pretty complex, all right," I stated.

That was usually a good one, too: get the insecure, inexperienced, easily intimidated auditing kids the public accounting firm sent out to do the field work thinking about whether or not they might've made a wrong calculation; get them guessing, doubting their own abilities.

Matthew Logan, for example, couldn't have been more than twenty-two, fresh out of university, fresh meat for the year-end client audit grind. He was small and compact, with curly brown hair and big brown eyes behind the glasses, a square, firm-jawed face. Clean-cut and no-nonsense, his pale blue suit was straight off the rack, his maroon striped tie and grey-striped shirt clashing as badly with the cheesecloth business suit as his shiny brown shoes.

But, unfortunately, what the guy lacked in experience and fashion sense, he made up for in confidence and number sense.

"I ran some salary figures through the program I created that replicates the company pension and dental deduction tables, and the results were off for five of the one hundred sampled employees – too high." He leaned forward in the uncomfortable plastic chair I'd provided to expedite our interview, keen as a knife at my throat.

I pursed my lips, tented my fingers. Time for Plan B: steering the conversation down audit trail memory lane until it's hopelessly lost, and time has expired on the interview. I smiled charmingly, familiarly. "One hundred employees? That's a pretty big sample size. In my day – when I was articling with Arthur Andersen – we sampled maybe thirty, then relied on our internal control testing results from the interim audit." It was also a suggestion. But he wasn't taking either bait.

"Interesting. Anyway, can you explain why Theo Vandemeer's pension contribution deduction was $74.25 for the semi-monthly pay period ended August 31, when according to my calculations it should have been $69.30, based on the deduction rate of 4.2% stipulated for his $1,650 gross pay salary bracket?"

A damn good question.

But young Matthew had an even better follow-up query. "And how come the correct amount of $69.30 was posted to the overall pension contribution general ledger account, while the excess $4.95 got credited to an account called," he checked his notes, as I mentally mouthed along, "Other Miscellaneous Administration."

That was the collecting G/L account for the surplus, fraudulent deductions that I periodically transferred to a numbered bank account I controlled, via an 'Administrative Fees' expenditure charge. Small sums add up fast when a company has more than two thousand employees.

Matthew set the payroll register down on my desk and picked his laptop up off the carpet. "Here, I'll show you my calculations on the spreadsheet I created."

The psychological tactics had failed; direct action was called for. I sprang up from my chair and strode around the desk and in back of the eager young auditing beaver, full cup of coffee in my hand. Then I stooped over Matthew's square shoulder, ostensibly to look at the computer screen. And 'accidentally' spilled the contents of my cup all over his keyboard. "Dammit!" I yelped. "Sorry about that!"

He jumped up out of the chair, warm coffee running off his shirt and pants and computer. I grabbed the machine out of his hands and shook it off upside down, helping the guy out. Accidentally again smacking it hard against the sharp corner of my desk a couple of times, cracking the cheapo laptop almost in two. "Dammit! Am I a Clumsy Carp today, or what!?" I shrugged my shoulders and grinned sheepishly, handing the auditor back his broken laptop buzzing its last breath. Taking his specially-created database with it.

I knew there was no time in the young man's payroll audit budget to recoup lost programs. He and his cohorts were due at another client next week.

Matthew stared morosely down at his busted computer, as I plucked some Kleenex out of a box and helpfully dabbed his damp Wal-Mart shirt and tie. This time truly accidentally popping one of his loose buttons open – thereby exposing a thick whorl of brown hair on his chest.

"Bear!" I breathed, gazing at the peeking clump of hair. Losing my composure for the first time during the Q&A. Hairy situations be damned, nothing gets my blood and cock pumping like a hairy man!

I thrust my Kleenexed hand right into Matthew's shirt, popping more buttons, finding more hair: a thick, rich coat of soft brown fur hidden beneath the cheesy dress shirt and buttoned-up collar, camouflaged by the thick grey stripes. There was a bear in there. And I went a-hunting.

"Uh, Mr. Purman ..."

"Doug," I murmured, popping all of his shirt buttons open with my shaking hands. Baring his chest, bringing the bear out of hibernation. The wadded Kleenex dropping unattended down to his bellybutton.

I spread his shirt wide and stared at the mass of follicled foliage on the young man's rising and falling chest. His sturdy pecs were absolutely blanketed, hair as brown and curly and thick as the stuff on his head, his pink nipples barely visible through the screening pelt; a heavy line of fur running out of the chest thatch and down his flat stomach and into his pants.

I swallowed, hard. And then dove my trembling hands into Matthew's thicket, clutching the fine-threaded whorls. Openly rubbing the guy's hairy chest, petting his coat. He moaned softly, his sharp, brown eyes misting, blinking behind his lenses.

That's when I remembered that there was a man behind the beautiful, bountiful fur – an impressionable young auditing man who had the goods on this shady embezzler. The popped gears of my mind tumbled back into place, meshed. And I full-out implemented Plan D: to fully satisfy everyone's needs – both sexually and auditally.

I fingered my way through the brown brush and found Matthew's hardened nipples and gently pinched them, rolled them, precisely unlocking the combination to his accounting heart. He groaned, his eyelids fluttering. I pressed my advantage home, cupping his flushed, furry pecs and dipping my head down and burrowing my tongue through his chest hair, licking one of his nipples.

171

"Oh, Mr. ... Doug!" he gasped, grabbing onto my shoulders.

The bear was snared. And I wasn't about to let him go without taking his pelt.

I swirled my tongue all around the one stiff, straining nipple – as best I could through the protective covering – and then the other one. Spit-shining his rubbery, pink buds up even harder and higher with my long, strong tongue. It was heavy going; just the way I like it.

Then I caught a nipple and a mouthful of hair between my lips and sucked on the blossomed bud. Matthew's body jerked in my clutching, coveting hands, his own hands gone damp on my shoulders. I held tight to his all-season coat, jumping my head over and sucking on his other nipple. Pulling hard and wet and hot on the rigid jutters, mouth full of tangled, ticklish hair, fingers entwining and tugging on his woven pelt.

He almost tumbled over backwards with my ardor. But I held him up by his chest hair, and my mouth. Sucking, tonguing, biting; mincing that thick, wet, matted fur around in my mouth with delight, chewing on it. My cock a hot, pulsing rod in my pinstriped pants. I glanced down and saw that Matthew was tenting his own trousers, just about splitting the seams on the discountwear. It was time to taking this heated meeting to the next level.

Lifting my head, but holding tight to the hair on his chest, I kissed Matthew on the lips. Soft and dry and questioning. Then hard and wet and demanding.

His full, red lips were as soft and springy as his lovely whorls of hair, and I devoured them. Sucking out what little resistance the young man had left in him. He moaned, his breath hot and humid and spearmint-flavored in my face and mouth.

Now, I'm forty-five years old, with thinning black hair up top and thick black hair all over, a bit of a spread. But I'm still in fairly, bearly good shape, am still quite attractive to the same sex; obviously so to Matthew. Because he impetuously flung his arms around my burly body and kissed me right back, eagerly moving his sweet lips against mine.

I pulled off his glasses and dumped them onto my desk, obscuring his vision, his reason for being there, even more. Then I regrabbed a second fistful of chest hair and thrust my tongue into his mouth and thrashed it around. Communicating to the lad in an excited language far removed from dull, dry accounting and auditing jargon. And his tongue responded eagerly, sliding against mine, speaking his delight.

We swirled our slippery, sensitive, red appendages together over and over. My hands all over his chest, fingers weaving urgently into his fur.

Then I pulled back. He stared at me with glassy eyes, panting. As I tore off my shirt and tie, ripped open my belt, shoved down my pants and briefs. Revealing to the young cub even more hair than he sported. Not as thick and concentrated in one spot, but spread lush and long and jet-black all over my chest, arms and legs; the wildly unkempt bush between my legs sprouting a smooth, pink, seven-inch stem capped by a purple-shaded bulb.

Matthew gaped. Then imitated. Stripping off his own tie and shirt, skinning down his pants and staid, grey shorts. His solid arms and legs were only lightly fairy-dusted with brown hair, compared to the growth on his chest, but his pubes were as long and unshorn as mine, his cock long and hard and pink like mine, with a meaty hood. The hair on his chest and body and balls glinted auburn in the afternoon sunlight. Which is when I remembered to hastily shutter the window.

Then I walked in behind Matthew, cockily bobbing, and kicked the chair out of the way. I grabbed onto his cock, sliding my own hard-on up and into his rounded butt cheeks, pressing it and my body close. He grunted appreciatively, as I squeezed my hot, hairy body tight against his burning body, stroking his pulsing prick with one hand while I petted his pelted chest with the other. Sinking my throbbing rod in between his soft, plump, peach-fuzzed buttocks and gently frotting.

No words were spoken, no questions asked. This was a sensual summing up, an accounting for good taste. Our bodies melded together, shimmering skin to skin.

I rubbed his tufted chest and rubbed up against him, letting him get a good feel of my hairy torso and loins against his bare back and buttocks. And he reached back and locked his sweaty paws onto my ass, gripping and squeezing the thick, downy flesh. It was my turn to groan – into his reddened ear – grinding my pulsating pole into his heated butt cleavage.

174

I kissed the scruffy back of his neck, licked aside his curls and in behind his ears, nuzzling the Pert-scented hair on his head. As I pumped his cheeks and his cock, rubbing and rubbing and tangling my fingers in his chest-coat.

But time was running short – I had a three o'clock with an IRS agent, and I'd need plenty of strength and all of my cunning for that session. A bear's gotta cover his tracks, or he'll end up in a cage.

So, I let go of Matthew's beating chest and cock and grabbed a tube of lube out of a filing cabinet drawer. I quickly greased my gun, Matthew's hairy crack.

"Oooo!" he gulped, when my slick fingers slid in between his quivering cheeks and rubbed him the right way.

I gripped my slickened dong at the furry base, and Matthew – bright boy that he was – bent forward and reached back, spreading his fleshy butt cheeks, exposing his browneye. His gloryhole was hairy and puckered like I like 'em. And I hit it. Hard. Driving my gleaming hood into his starfish and squishing around for a moment, then bursting through resisting ring and plunging into anus proper.

"That's the ticking and bopping Daddy likes!" I growled, grabbing onto the young man's hips and pushing forward, sinking my cock deep into his hot, tight chute.

He grunted and gripped the desk, fully impaled on my stake. I pulled back, gliding almost all the way out of his sucking ass, watching and feeling his butt tendrils stroke my buzzing shaft. Before plunging back in again, hairy balls to the hairy walls. I pumped my hips, fucking the groaning man.

But as electrifying as the anal-cock stimulation was, I wanted still more tactile sensation. So I grabbed Matthew around the chest and hauled him back up against me, sliding my fingers into his fur and holding on, as I slammed my cock up his ass.

"Yeah, Doug! Fuck me, Doug!" the bred-in-the-bone-to-be conservative and objective auditor cried. Getting boned by a fellow bear – a more compelling fraternity. He arched his back against my hairy torso, his fur-plated body shuddering in rhythm to my urgent cock-thrusts.

I mouthed the hair on the nape of his neck, felt up the hair rug on his chest, pounding cock into his hair-rimmed chute. The rasping of our frenzied breathing, the smacking of my clenched thighs against his rippling butt cheeks, filling the sweat and sex-funked office. The heat and the pressure rising, mounting, towering; my flapping balls boiling and flying cock surging.

Matthew frantically fisted his own prick, matching the bum-splitting tempo of my pistoning dick. He desperately twisted his head around, and our tongues flailed together. Before all pretense of auditor-client impartiality was blown away for good – my plundering cock exploding in Matthew's ass, blasting his chute. Matthew echoing my cries of joy, jacking bursts of heated jizz out of his cock.

I almost tore the young man's chest hair out by the roots, wild, wicked orgasm rocking me back on my heels. My cock jumped and pumped in his shivering ass, as I blindly, ecstatically poured white-hot semen down the bear's anus for what seemed like forever. Matthew jerking and jumping up onto his toes with his own blazing orgasm.

It was a bit of a surprise, then, when after reconstituting ourselves in our business attire, Matthew said, "About those pension and dental deductions, Mr. Purman ..."

The guy was one hardnosed auditor.

But I played hardball, too; as well as balling hard. A tiny camera I'd attached to the sprinkler head mounted on the ceiling of my office had captured the entire bodily, unbusinesslike transaction. To be used against auditors like Matthew for the purpose of compromising their careers, if they didn't compromise their positions.

I haven't spent a day in prison or on the unemployment line yet. While enjoying close, intimate relationships with a whole host of hot and hairy auditors and agents.

F***ING MUSCLE-BOYS
By Landon Dixon

I spanked the ball off the wall down low. Jonah dived for it way too late, as it ricocheted on by. He did a sliding bellyflop into the glass door, nose-first. 11 points. My game, set and match.

"Good play," Jonah gasped from his stomach, trying to save what face he had that wasn't suffering floor-burn. He rolled over onto his back, looking like a beached whale in his sweated-see-through white shirt and shorts, his stomach heaving up and down. He held up his hand.

It took both of my skinny arms and all of my long back to hoist the guy up to his sneakers. Then we exited the high-walled campus handball court and walked down the green-carpeted hallway that led to the locker rooms. We heard the grunting and groaning, the clanking of metal plates, of some dedicated student or staff member working out in the weight room off to the side.

"Some fucking muscle-boy just can't stop pumping up, eh? Even at this late hour on a Sunday," I commented to Jonah, as we strolled into the men's locker room wiping sweat off our faces with white towels. "Afraid his precious muscles will atrophy before the big game."

Jonah giggled. "Yeah. Those muscle-heads have to lift all the time, or they'll lose their pretty physiques. They're slaves to their bodies, those cement-heads." He stopped at a locker and pulled off his wet t-shirt, letting his hairy stomach bounce free.

Except for me and Jonah, and a couple of athletic center staff members hunkered down in the snack room, and the guy peaking his bis and strafing his pecs in the weight room, the gym complex was all-but deserted. These fucking muscle-boys were always preening around, though, so insecure about their bodies and so fragile of psyche that they had to show off their muscles constantly to any man or mirror they came into contact with. That's why Jonah and I liked to keep to the handball courts and stationary bike and treadmill room − to avoid all that ridiculous narcissism. And because our 'bookish' physiques didn't quite measure up, as well, of course.

Jonah dropped his sodden shirt into his backpack along with his gloves and skinned down his soaked shorts, letting his big, pale butt cheeks flop out. "I'm going to grab a shower and then get me a snack." He turned to look at me, so I got a good view of his flabby young man-boobs. "Sound good?"

I'd only known Jonah a couple of weeks. He was my lab partner in our advanced chemistry class, a curly-haired guy with a moonface and dimpled chipmunk cheeks, deep-set blue eyes and multiple chins. He was smart as a whip, but not a sight for sore four-eyes.

He grinned lasciviously at me, idly fingering a swollen pink nipple buried in his brown chest hair. His

180

wettened white briefs bulged with more than just cafeteria-fed lower midriff.

We both turned our heads and glanced down the aisle formed by the double-row of grey lockers, when we heard someone drop a gym bag down onto the polished wooden bench that bisected the aisle, down at the end. It was obviously the same guy who'd been blasting his quads and shredding his abs in the weight room.

A huge, black man, our age, dressed in a purple mesh muscle-shirt and tiny pair of blue shorts. He turned his head and looked sideways at the full-length mirror affixed to the wall at the end of the aisle. And then he gripped his right wrist with his left hand and curled his right arm, flexing a massive bicep for inspection and admiration.

"Would you look at that fucking muscle-boy," I hissed. "He can't keep his hands and eyes off himself for even one minute."

Jonah sneered, sucking in his gut and chest as best as he could. "Yeah, what a show-off." He looked back at me. "So, how 'bout that shower and some eats? Maybe a beer or two at the pub, too." He winked suggestively.

I kept my eyes glued to the posing muscle-boy. A lot of these dudes were well under six feet, little guys trying to compensate for what they lacked in God-given height with man-made and chemical-induced width. But this collegian was at least six-foot-four, if not taller. And from what I could see from my distant vantage point, reflected in the mirror, he was a pretty good-looking guy, too – close-cropped dark hair and large brown eyes, smooth face with strong nose and cleft chin, high cheekbones. No pimples all over his face and back, no receding hair and chin lines.

He teeth flashed white in the mirror as he flexed, his right leg bending so that his bunched quad clenched, like he was up on stage being judged, competing against a group of fellow fucking muscle-boys. "Uh, no, you go ahead," I mouthed to Jonah, watching the guy at the end of the aisle.

Jonah yanked his red polo shirt and green chinos out of the locker and jerked them on, then slammed the door shut and scooped up his backpack. "See you around sometime – in class, maybe," he grated, striding off as fast as his stumpy legs would carry him.

"Fucking muscle-boys," I breathed, fixated on the guy pumping up in the mirror. "Can't let it rest for a minute. Always worried they're losing muscle mass."

The big man released his wrist and straightened out his arm and leg. Then he turned back to his gym bag on the bench and stripped off his mesh shirt. He tossed the shirt onto the bench, dug around in his bag. The huge muscles on his broad shoulders and long arms twitched and jumped. He pulled a clear plastic bottle out of the bag and swung around to face the mirror again, squirted some baby oil or something onto a wide palm and started smoothing the liquid over his humped pecs with a large hand.

"Holy fuck," I murmured to myself, shaking my head and sidling closer to the right-side bank of lockers to get a better view of the guy in the mirror. "This fucking muscle-boy's going to go through his whole fucking routine. Oiling himself up and putting on a one-man show. Fucking muscle-boy prima donnas."

He rubbed the oil onto his popping chest, his ribbed stomach and rugged shoulders, smearing his hands all over his muscles. His mammoth upper body gleamed, his serrated, cable-like muscle fibers clearly separating and standing out on his mushroomed torso. Until he reached around at his back, and his sinew-thickened arms could take his huge hands only halfway up.

I walked down the aisle toward the chiseled ebony giant, my white shorts and shirt plastered to my quivering body. "Fucking muscle-bound muscle-boy. Can't even reach every part of his body, he's so bloated with muscles."

The guy couldn't see me approaching in the mirror, his mountainous physique blocking his view. His glutes at the back were even more heaped than his pecs at the front, just as taut and powerful. They clenched under the skin-tight material of his shorts, as he strained to reach his upper back with his hands. His lats blossomed like bat wings, rear delts roiling python-like under his polished, black velvet skin.

"N-Need some help?"

He twisted his tree-stump of a neck around and looked at me. His brown eyes shone and his teeth flashed a dazzling white again. He held up the bottle of baby oil. "You got my back? Hey, thanks, man."

His voice was just as deep and masculine as his overblown muscles. This muscle-boy, at least, didn't squeak like a little elementary kid.

He turned back to the mirror and fisted his hands and planted them on his narrow hips, fanned out his lats in an easy flex. I tipped and squeezed the bottle, jetting out oil onto my hand and the floor. I set the bottle down on the bench, then slapped my shaking hands onto the guy's gargantuan, spread upper body and rubbed.

"That hits the spot," he rumbled in appreciation. "Name's Terrance. Thanks for the help."

Fucking muscle-boys always needed help, despite their ferocious appearance. "B-Ben!" I blurted.

I swirled my hands all over the big man's upper back, dripping oil from my twitching fingers, feeling the warm, smooth skin, the cords of steel wound tight beneath. I tried to dig my fingers in, to little avail. This fucking muscle-boy was a hard-body, for sure; he'd built a protective armored shell around himself to shield his fragile ego and feeble mind, no doubt.

"I'm an education major, how about you?"

"S-S-Science."

He boldly skinned down his shorts.

I stared at his bare boulder butt cheeks, my fingers clawing at his flared traps up-above.

"You're good with your hands, man."

I glanced up, and his eyes met mine in the mirror. He was grinning again. He looked down, and I followed with my eyes. I stared at the long, thick, licorice-black cock dangling down from his shaved loins, over his big, hairless balls.

"Fuck!" I whispered, gaping.

Most of these fucking muscle-boys had thumb-dicks, at best. Another reason they plated themselves with ludicrous amounts of muscle, to cover up their shortcomings.

I instinctively reached around and grasped Terrance's veined shaft with my slippery fingers. He grunted. I gulped. His huge cock stirred in my cupping hand, surged between my clasping fingers. This fucking muscle-boy was more than just protein and arrogance, I had to admit.

"Feels good," he growled, watching my blazingly pale hand shift up and down on his deep-purple cock in the mirror. "Pump it up, Ben."

I was watching, too, and feeling; pressing closer to Terrance's heated, sculpted, nude body, his swelling cock filling my hand and stretching my fingers. My own throbbing erection touched up against his rock-hard ass, then slid and pulsated in between his curved, carved butt-mounds.

I stroked his cock with more strength, tightening my grip on the awesome appendage as it rose up and jutted out. He spasmed his buttocks, clutching my cock with his glutes. I pumped the guy, back and front.

I pulled harder and faster, thrust quicker and more urgently. His cock engorged and elongated to at least nine glistening inches in my gliding hand; my own cock straining steel-hard in my shorts and his butt cleft, buffing his crack and ass walls. I hugged up against the big man, humping into him.

He couldn't take too much of a good thing, though (or maybe he just wanted even better). Because he slowly pivoted around to face me, popping my cock out of his ass and his own out of my hand. These fucking muscle-boys are notoriously quick to go off, plenty of self-control when it comes to diet and exercise, but precious little when it comes to desire. Terrance placed his hands on my shoulders and pushed me down to my knees on the carpet, at his cock.

I gazed into the gaping slit on his bulbous black hood. I glanced up at him. He smiled down at me, every muscle on his body-beautiful tensed, including the most beautiful muscle of all. I slid my lips over his crown and mouthed the meaty, mushroomed tip of his monster cock.

His knees buckled and his hands dropped down onto my head. I consumed more of his enormous erection, pushing my head forward and stretching my lips out and opening my mouth up wider; swallowing inch after pulsing inch of that dark, delicious, vein-ribboned dong.

My eyes watered and my nostrils flared, my face filling up with heat and cock. Saliva drooled out of the corners of my mouth and snot bubbled out of my nose. I kept moving inexorably forward, though, letting Terrance's cock slide into my mouth like a snake into a pond, just as wet and warm. Until the man's hood touched the back of my throat and bent down, his shaft plunging my windpipe.

He shuddered and groaned, muscles jumping, fingers digging into my hair. These fucking muscle-boys are always blown away by my capacity for cock. I hadn't met a one yet I couldn't down, although Terrance's was certainly the biggest and best. My lips kissed up against his groin and I pushed out my tongue and licked at his sack, my cheeks and throat ballooned with meat.

I rolled my teary eyes upward and looked into his slitted eyes. He pushed me back, rocked me forward on my knees, helping me deep-throat him. I sucked tight and moist on his cock, my arms dangling down at my sides in sweet surrender, my throat and lips and tongue working. His sack slapped against my chin, the musky scent of the super he-man buried balls-deep in my face filling my nose and making my head spin. Until he shoved me back so hard his cock sprang out of my mouth like a sea-creature surfacing, flinging saliva and pre-cum.

He helped me up to my feet, then down onto my back on the bench. These fucking muscle-boys, they always have to see themselves in action, so in love with their own bodies. Terrance straddled the bench and my head, facing the mirror. I snapped at his dripping cock spearing out over my face. But he lowered his sack down into my open mouth, giving me his balls to feed on, looking at his own jutting, slathered cock jabbing out into the mirror.

I swallowed his sack, taking all of the heavy, tight-wrinkled pouch into my mouth. Terrance grunted and jerked up above me. He swarmed his hands all over his swollen chest, strumming his pitch-black nipples, pinching and pulling on the pointed pair. As I tugged on his sack with my lips and swabbed his balls with my tongue, inhaling the essence of the man deep into my lungs.

He jumped forward, popping his balls out of my mouth when I'd just started really chewing on them. Terrance lowered his ass down to my face, wanting me to eat that sensuous part of him. I reached up and grabbed onto his buttocks, felt the thick muscles convulse under my fingers, staring into the dark, deep cleft in between. He dipped his ass lower, and I stuck out my tongue and striped his crack, wet-stroking the smooth, sensitive, vulnerable stretch of skin that bisected his rockpile buttocks. He vibrated, his cock straining almost straight up into the air and staying stiff at that angle. As I licked his luscious crack.

His cock and balls had tasted wonderful, his ass even better. I lapped in between his butt cheeks with wide, dragging tongue-strokes, clutching his spasming mounds. Every inch of these fucking muscle-boys was groomed, and this guy's butt cleavage was no exception. I swirled my tongue-tip around his sweet, puckered asshole, and then spiraled it right inside.

Terrance shuddered and grabbed onto his cock for support, stroked the dusky pole, working his massed pecs and rigid nipples with his other hand. I corkscrewed his anus to a depth of two inches, then rimmed his ring and painted his crack all over again.

He suddenly jumped off my face. Then he lifted me up and turned me over, positioning me onto my hands and knees on the bench, facing the mirror. My tongue lolled out with no butt-cleft to bathe, my hands now gripping wood rather than buttocks. Terrance loomed up behind me in the mirror, straddling the bench again, he ripped down my shorts. I felt pressure on my own asshole – something soft and thick squishing against my pucker.

The big guy's beefy, lubed cockhead burst through and engorged my ass ring, the man-mountain plugged into me again – at the most sensitive of sex openings now. His eyes locked onto mine in the mirror, as his hood plowed into my ass and his slickened shaft surged into my chute.

These fucking muscle-boys, I mentally screamed getting stuffed, they always have to try to dominate you! And Terrance was doing one hell of a job, his humungous cock stretching my anus and swelling my ass like nothing I'd ever felt before, jamming me full of sensation. His battering-ram barged into my chute up to the balls, leaving me gasping for air, my eyes hanging out. So help me, I thought I felt his hood on the back of my tongue.

He gripped my waist and rutted his embedded cock around in my electrified ass. Then he pumped his hips, rocking me to and fro on the bench to the pounding beat of his pistoning cock penetrating the absolute depths of my anus. He moved with pneumatic strength. I could only take it and feel it and stare in the mirror, watching the muscleman hammer me up the ass with his sledge.

He built up the pressure until I was leaking saliva and pre-cum, bouncing back and forth on his piledriver. And then, he turned the tables on me again. He rammed his cock full-length up my chute and then spun me around, so that I was flat on my back on the bench again. Terrance clutched my trembling, pasty-white thighs to his gleaming dark chest and thrust with his hips – fucking me face-on now.

I rolled my head around on the bench with delight, at the man's absolute mercy, held up by his powerful arms and split in two by his powerful cock. I grabbed onto my own bouncing cock and desperately jacked. And I was so far gone, so fucked up the ass with feeling, that I blasted sperm with the first tug on my cock.

I jerked like a piked fish, jetting sheer joy out of my dong and all over my face. Hot, sticky semen splashed into my open mouth and splattered onto my outstretched tongue, my body burning and cock blazing; anus seared inferno by Terrance's poured molten iron.

He was glaring straight ahead into the mirror, the fucking muscle-boy watching me spasm and spray and stripe myself, taking self-satisfaction in my uproarious orgasm. Watching his own sweat-sheened muscles buck and clutch and quiver, his shining cock spike my convulsing ass.

Then he grunted, and his eyelids fluttered, his eyes losing focus. He ripped his cock out of my ass, leaving my hole gaping and gasping, dropping me down flat on the bench. He rushed forward and plunged his cock into my open mouth. His big body jerked, repeatedly; heated semen spurted down my throat, repeatedly.

I stared up at the man, watching his awesome muscles vibrate to the snapping point, still frantically pulling ropes of shooting sperm out of my own cock. He flooded my mouth with his torrent of ecstasy, and I eagerly swallowed and swallowed and swallowed.

He bent down and tenderly kissed me when it was finally all over, tasting his own cum on my tongue and my cum on my lips. That's when I thought, these fucking muscle-boys, hard on the outside and soft on the inside. He probably wants to cuddle now, have me hold him and tell him how great he was.

But, instead, Terrance stood erect and said, "See you around, man. Maybe we'll workout again sometime." He swung away from me and the bench and strode off to the shower room all by himself.

In all the short, sexy years I'd been fucked by the muscle-boys, this was the best one yet. "This fucker's actually a pretty good guy," I sighed with contentment.

GROUP PROJECT
By Landon Dixon

"I suppose you're wondering why I called you all here today?"

It was an old joke, but still a good one. Shawn and Rafael laughed, as Connor followed up his gag by banging a spoon on the cafeteria table, like he was calling the meeting to order.

Only Justin didn't laugh. The small, tightly-wound, eighteen-year-old redhead with the horn-rimmed glasses and blazing brown eyes impatiently jumped forward in his chair and said, "Well, I guess we'd better get started. We only have six weeks to come up with a product and a marketing plan. We're going to have to work hard, log some long hours after class and on weekends. I figure ..."

But his cheery speech of exhortation was lost on his marketing classmates. Rafael was busy texting away on his cellphone. Connor was yelling and waving at a group of equally well-built and boisterous young men carrying loaded food trays into the cafeteria dining area. While Shawn was doodling in a notebook.

Justin gritted his straight, white teeth that were a little worn down at the edges (like his fingernails), his boyish face flaming pink with frustration. He was a high achiever, used to getting good marks and getting his way, academically. Full of drive and ambition, scared of failure and enjoyment. He'd been top of his class at his small, exclusive, suburban high school three years running, where his intellectual prowess and incredible work ethic had been rewarded, his social ineptitude overlooked.

But this was first-year university, at a large, diverse campus, and Justin was having a hard time adjusting, with the college's emphasis on creating 'well-rounded' individuals; with the wide array of group projects that seemed to form an awful lot of his course content in the Management program.

He'd always hated group projects. In group projects, you had to rely on other people – the other members of your group. You were supposed to get along with your fellow students and use everybody's special skills to produce the best group effort and result (two or five heads being better than one, in other words). In theory. In actuality, whenever Justin had run up against this groupthink nemesis in high school, he'd always ended up doing most, if not all, of the work. He just didn't trust his 'groupies' to do the job right. Who could carry out the assignment better than the star student alone, after all?

But going solo wasn't possible now – not with the heavy course load Justin was packing in his inaugural semester, coupled with the extensive project expectations of his marketing prof. Justin had to get his group mates organized and working, everyone contributing and

194

collaborating; or he'd be dragged down into the horrific depths of grade B or C shame with the rest of them.

Compounding Justin's apparent problem was the diverse nature of the group he'd been assigned to. Rafael – a tall, thin, brown-eyed, brown-haired young man with a loose mouth and sensuous lips, mocha skin and casual manner – was in the Arts faculty, taking marketing as an elective. While Connor, a huge, loud, farmer-tanned, buzz cut blond with cornflower blue eyes and jughead ears, was majoring in football, with a minor in beer bashes. And even though quiet, doe-eyed, dark-skinned, slender and supple Shawn was enrolled in Management, like Justin, the guy seemed more interested in sketching and doodling, making with the colored pencils and paper rather than the laptop and textbooks. First year college was always a miasma of mentalities.

Justin was the only one interested in garnering good grades and a good job when he graduated. Or so it seemed to the academic savant, but socially backward young man, as he hypercritically studied the other members of his group where they sat at the back of the cafeteria.

Connor abruptly lurched to his feet, almost capsizing the folding table on top of Justin and Shawn who were sitting across from him. He lumbered over to his football playmates, and they locked hands in greeting and then huddled together, barking out banter that echoed throughout the cavernous room. Rafael punched his cellphone screen with a slender digit and put the mobile chatterbox to his ear, started conversing in hushed tones to the exclusion of the rest of the remaining group. Shawn smiled at the steam billowing out of Justin's burning ears, flipped his notebook to a fresh page and began sketching out a picture of an exasperated boyish physiognomy in shades of red and pink.

"We've got to get organized, figure out what we're going to do and who's going to do it!" Justin desperately instructed to no one paying attention. "We only have six weeks, and I was projecting an A+ in this course," he lamented, his dreams of a perfect 4.0 grade point average already slipping away.

# # # # #

Justin scheduled another group meeting for the end of the week. Even that took some doing – corralling his divergent classmates together in the name of scholarship, and scholarships. He booked a study room on the fifth floor of the Student Union Building for four-thirty on the Friday, banned electronic devices of all kinds (other than his one Nanny-netted laptop), and forbade any mention of outside activities or gossip not germane to the group project.

Justin stood at the door of the small, isolated room in the all-but deserted building, examining each group member as they unenthusiastically shuffled inside. Then he closed the door and locked it. Four ten-page folios containing the meeting agenda and Justin's proposed project synopsis were waiting on the round, wooden table as Connor, Rafael and Shawn sat down.

"Hey, why'd we have to meet on a Friday, anyway?" Connor protested loudly, again. "You know, we're the only dorks still on campus, dudes." He looked around at the others, then lowered his huge head when he met Justin's glare.

"This way," Justin declared, taking a seat, "we can get everything organized so that we can all work on our part of the project over the weekend."

"Who got expelled and elected this guy group leader?" Rafael objected mildly.

"We do have six weeks," Shawn pointed out.

"Five weeks and three days," Justin countered, opening his folio and getting down to business. "Now, we need a product and a marketing plan. Any ideas?"

Rafael shrugged. Shawn squinted. Connor blew out his cheeks and blubbered his lips.

Justin sighed and flipped to the first page of the document he'd typed up and copied for the group. Frustratingly, no one followed his lead. "I think ..."

"I gotta go to the can," Connor interrupted, bouncing the table up with his heavy thighs as he got to his feet. He trundled to the door and tore it open, ambled down the fifth floor hallway without looking back.

Rafael followed after the big guy, more gracefully, in search of a drink of water, so he claimed. While Shawn flipped his folio upside down and opened up the back cover, started doodling on the last page of the document Justin had labored long and hard to create.

Justin leapt to his feet and yelped, "What's with you guys!? Don't you want to get good grades!? Succeed!?"

Shawn looked up at him and smiled softly, his green eyes warm and gentle. "College is about more than just getting good grades, Justin."

"Yes! It's about getting a good-paying job after you graduate – with good grades!" He scrubbed his damp palms on his tan pants, his fingers twitching and face reddening.

"Haven't you ever heard of the 'college experience'?" Shawn asked, going back to his drawing. "You know, socializing, making new friends, trying and discovering new things, having new experiences."

"I've never failed anything in my life, and I don't intend to start now!" Justin ranted and panted on, ignoring his classmate.

Shawn put down his pink pencil and picked up a red, shaded his sketch, glancing up at Justin. "It's all about making 'contacts' – to put it in a marketing vernacular – that can last you a lifetime. Getting to know others and yourself a lot better."

"I'll demand new group members," Justin huffed and puffed, pounding his small fist into his palm as he rapidly paced. "Or ... I'll postpone marketing until next semester. Or ... maybe I can do it all by myself, if I only sleep three hours a night."

"Hey, Justin, calm down – take a look at this." Shawn held up the full-page rough draft he'd completed.

Justin glanced at it, then stopped in his tracks. His eyes lost their maniacal focus, as he stared at the sketch.

The picture represented in pink and red was of a young man who bore a striking resemblance to Justin. The boyishly-handsome man was strikingly nude, however, his large, pink cock jutting out from his ginger-hued loins. The joyously erect tool appeared as eager as the look in the boy's wide eyes behind his horn-rimmed glasses. Shawn had titled the provocative sketch 'Hungry for Knowledge,' at the bottom.

Justin gulped and plopped down in his chair, gaping at the naked rendering of himself.

Shawn slid his free hand across the table and over top of one of Justin's splayed hands. "That's what I see beneath all the anxiety and bluster," the amateur artist explained, squeezing Justin's hand. "College is about sexual education, too, you know."

Justin's widened eyes jumped from the sketch into Shawn's shining eyes. His Adam's apple bobbed wildly again, his face torching redder, his palm bleeding wetter under Shawn's warm, covering hand.

"Let's go see if we can Rafael and Connor," Shawn said. Then he added with a grin, "I think I might know what they're up to – our group mates."

He led Justin out of the room by the hand.

Justin's full, red lips trembled, but he was speechless for a change, compliant, academic achievement forgotten. He followed behind Shawn on tottering legs, guided by his fellow student's clasping hand. He stared down at Shawn's taut, mounded butt cheeks in the man's black track pants, watching the pair clench and quiver; Justin easily led astray when the human contact was this unexpectedly close.

The pair travelled down the hushed hallway to the open doors of the student lounge at the end, looked inside. Connor and Rafael were sprawled out on one of the modular brown couches that bordered two walls of the room, their arms around one another and their lips locked together. They were kissing, frenching, fondling, passionately and unabashedly.

Justin quivered at the sight of the two men going at it tongues and lips and hands; then jumped, when Shawn let go of his hand and placed one hand on Justin's crotch and the other on Justin's butt, started rubbing the startled young man front and back.

Rafael pulled away from Connor's chewing mouth and pushed up the big blond's grey sweatshirt. He cupped Connor's humped pecs with his lean hands, then swirled his stuck-out pink tongue around one squeezed-up red nipple, the other cherry blossom. Making Connor groan and writhe. As Shawn warmly rubbed in between Justin's tensed butt cheeks and over the rapidly tensing bulge in the front of the boy's pants. Justin swallowed the saliva that suddenly filled his mouth, his glutes and groin shimmering with sensation, the rest of his waifish body flooding with tingling heat.

Rafael dragged his glistening tongue down Connor's heaving, ribbed stomach, sliding the big guy's blue team sweatpants down as he did so. Connor's cock sprang out into the open, as pumped and slab-like as the rest of his body. Rafael laced the shaft with his long fingers, poured his plush lips over the beefy tip, capturing bare, beating cock hand and mouth.

"Fuckin' right!" Connor bellowed, bucking on the couch, plunging more of his thick cock into Rafael's accommodating mouth.

Justin blinked his eyes for the first time in what seemed like hours, watching and feeling – body, sight and soul – the enormously erotic action. His cock was as wickedly rigid as Connor's under Shawn's sensuous rubbing, his buttocks trembling as excitedly as Connor's body beneath Shawn's petting fingers. He gasped like Connor grunted, when Rafael dipped his glossy head down lower and inhaled almost all of the rest of Connor's sledge.

"Enjoying yourself?" Shawn breathed in Justin's beet-red ear over the blood pounding therein. He pumped his deft fingers along Justin's crack and cock in rhythm to Rafael sucking on Connor's cock.

Justin eagerly bobbed his head, just like Rafael.

Shawn grinned. "I told you college wasn't all work and no play. Why don't we collaborate more closely with our classmates – in a real group effort?"

Justin didn't object at all to the redirection of his surging energies. Thinking with the swollen head of his cock now, thoughts decidedly non-academic (unless you were enrolled in the sex therapy option, of course). He let Shawn lead him over to the other two men. They greeted the pair's intrusion on their down-time enthusiastically, Rafael popping his mouth off Connor's cock and hand-pumping the slick, hardened member as he said, "Room for two more."

Justin felt his clothes melt off his burning body, and before he knew it, the whole group was naked, a sexy foursome prepped and perved for learnin' of the carnal variety. Shawn lay back next to Connor on the couch, pulling Justin down in between his spread legs like Rafael was positioned in between Connor's legs.

Justin stared at the dark-chocolate tool laid out hard and twitching on Shawn's flat stomach. He glanced at Rafael gripping Connor's blond-dusted balls now and wet-vaccing Connor's pulsating cock again. Then he looked back at Shawn's manly appendage, the tight, pube-pebbled sack beneath. He grasped Shawn's balls with one hand, picked up the mushroomed hood of Shawn's cock with his lips and sucked on the man's deep-purple cap.

"Now, you're really catching on," Shawn moaned, grasping Justin's red head with one hand and rolling his own pointed, pitch-black nipples with the other.

Justin thrilled at the feel of Shawn's hefty sack and shifting balls between his fingers, at the taste and texture of Shawn's beefy, bulbous hood between his lips. He happily sucked more of Shawn's cock into his mouth, swallowing thick, vein-corded shaft and then tugging on it. He squeezed Shawn's balls, vacced Shawn's cock; he and Rafael groping and blowing the pair of groaning men almost in unison. Group coordination at last!

The two sucked men soon shifted around and sprawled out flat on their backs on the couch, pulled the two cocksuckers over top of them, backwards. Connor grabbed onto Rafael's dangling, tan meat and stuffed it into his big mouth. He exuberantly shunted his head up and down, sucking on the pipe from below as Rafael sucked on his cock from above, sixty-nine-style.

Justin, in the same sexual position with Shawn, gripped the shaft of the cock he'd just polished to gleaming with his saliva and mouth. Then he suddenly jerked, jolted by the blissful impact of Shawn's soft lips kissing his slit, the man's slim fingers wrapping around the base of his raging boner. Justin quickly dropped his mouth back over Shawn's edible cock, muffling the pleasure-filled moan that rose up from his balls.

He re-consumed half of Shawn's dong in the moist, heated confines of his satin-lined mouth. As Shawn subsumed almost all of Justin's throbbing erection in his wet-velvet mouth, making the young man's bare body jump with joy.

Justin sucked. Shawn sucked. Connor and Rafael sixty-nined, too. The lusty male sounds of grunting and gasping, slurping and snorting, filled the student lounge. All four men earnestly putting in a concentrated effort that aroused and astounded Justin like never before in the midst of a group project.

And the dizzied young man was equally amazed at how well-prepared his group mates had come. Condoms were cracked open and applied to all straining cocks, then lube. Connor and Shawn sat back up slumped on the couch again, and Rafael and Justin straddled their waists now, their knees spraddling the couch cushions rather than the carpet. Justin watched with his mouth hanging open and his eyes hanging out, as Rafael reached back and grasped Connor's shining cock, stuck the tip into his asshole, then sat fully down on the other man's turgid member. Connor's guttural exclamation of pure pleasure, and the look of exquisite ecstasy on Rafael's pretty face, as cock plowed into anus, shook Justin to his loins. He couldn't wait to experience it himself, broaden his sexucational horizons with a blast.

He lifted up higher, gripped Shawn's gleaming cock in behind, looking into Shawn's smiling eyes. Then he squished latexed cap against resisting pucker, poked Shawn's cockhead through his ass ring with a shudder and sigh. And then he gritted his teeth and dropped his butt down flat on Shawn's thighs, filling his own ass entirely with another man's erection.

"Oh my ... Oh, Jesus!" Justin cried out, impaled on Shawn's pole. His anus blazed with the beating cock inside, his ass bloated to bursting, chute stuffed and stretched like never before.

Shawn reached up and grasped Justin's quivering pecs, pumped his hips. His cock glided back and forth inside Justin's ass, delighting the young man still more. Justin rocked to the anus-reaming rhythm, like Rafael on Connor; his rock-hard cock bouncing to keep pace.

But this wasn't a pairs program. It was a group project. The men lay down on the carpet, four a-spoon.

Shawn and Connor were at the ends, Rafael and Justin in the middle of the meats sandwich.

Justin felt Shawn's glorious cock split his cheeks and sink into his chute again. As he watched Rafael plunge his cock into Connor's beefy ass. The young man gripped his own cock and probed the bulbed tip in between Rafael's smooth, bubble cheeks. He poked pucker, resolutely pushed forward. And slowly, and extremely sensuously, his cockhead and then shaft plowed into Rafael's anus.

Justin was enveloped in erotic heat, his cock flaming vise-tight in another man's ass; another man's cock buried up his blazing butt. Shawn shoved the final two inches of Justin into Rafael with a thrust of his hips.

The four men moved together, fucking one another, Connor jacking. Clenched thighs spanked rippling butt cheeks, clawing hands clutching shoulders and chests, heavy breathing and sharp, tangy sweat and musky ball-scent filling the crackling air. The sexual pressure pumping and pumping and pumping up past the point of no return.

Justin wailed, "Ohmigod!" pounding his cock into Rafael's shuddering ass, wildly splashing his body against the man. He spasmed, shot sperm, awesome ecstasy exploding inside of him and his classmate's chute. He felt Shawn's fingernails bite into his shaking shoulders and Shawn's teeth sink into his corded neck, as that man violently convulsed against him and added liquid fire to the inferno already raging inside his anus.

Rafael and Connor came with the pair, all four group members letting loose with their members. A meeting of like minds and bodies; the happiest ending to a group session Justin had ever experienced.

# # # # #

Their product was called "Conjugal Campus Cabins" – love shacks on wheels for the privacy-challenged college dorm crowd, rented by the hour, night or weekend, gay-friendly and group-accommodating. Sex toys, condoms, lubes and movies sold separately. The accompanying marketing plan was a product of hard work and even harder practical application.

They scored an A on the group assignment. But for Justin, he'd scored so much more (and often). The young man fully immersed himself in the college experience, his horizons expanded beyond his wildest, wettest dreams. He realized just how important and exciting the social side of university was, coupled with the educational. The group dynamic worked perfectly for the young man now, both academically and anally.

g any underwear. "Excuse me," I said, having a hard time looking

ed by that bulge in his crotch, "but don't I know you?" "Maybe," h

of t   bout a m

Ray   God, you

er?   in?" he as

'Lik   s stronges

ody   e on Gree

he l   I ever sa

to t   any ideas?

ing   he same

coul   ery long t

rac   he swell.

with   e in store

go c   behind so

see u   in public

' he   vent to the

acy.   grabbed

d. I

raci   t, so firm

t, ha

h my   bing dick

ig, I   n cock, be

sound of unzipping filled the small space. I don't know who's hand

t before I knew it, I had his rod in my hand, and mine was in his. "

o do?" he asked, his tone challenging. I knew exactly, and sank to n

www.ingramcontent.com/pod-product-compliance
Lightning Source LLC
Chambersburg PA
CBHW051133020726
47501CB00005B/1482